D0052160

~ SEDUCTION IN THE CITY ~

OVERTIME IN THE BOSS'S BED

NICOLA MARSH

Hot days, hotter nights...

HARLEQUIN Presents

EXTRA

There are two great story collections from
Presents EXTRA for you to buy this month:

The **Greek Tycoons** collection
Legends are made of men like these!

The **Seduction in the City** collection
Hot days, hotter nights…

ISBN-13:978-0-373-52771-7

GREEK TYCOONS:

**#105 THE GREEK TYCOON'S
ACHILLES HEEL**
Lucy Gordon

**#106 THE POWER OF THE
LEGENDARY GREEK**
Catherine George

SEDUCTION IN THE CITY:

**#107 OVERTIME IN THE
BOSS'S BED**
Nicola Marsh

**#108 WILD FLING OR A
WEDDING RING?**
Mira Lyn Kelly

HPEATMIFC06

"Shall we start the interview?"

It was impossible to stand there and pretend only to view him as a prospective boss when she'd seen him naked.

"Yes, right. The interview."

Inwardly cringing at her awkward response, she dropped her hands to her sides, flexed her fingers, shook them out, mustered her best stage face.

"What do you want to know? My typing speed? PC skills? Microsoft literate? Multitasker?"

Heck, she was babbling, sounding more moronic by the second, while his expression remained impassive, his gaze focused on her with frightening clarity, and she suddenly knew she'd been a fool to mistake this man for anything other than an imperturbable, composed businessman who'd let nothing stand in the way of getting what he wanted.

"I need a P.A."

And she needed money desperately.

A win-win for them both.

If she could just forget the fact she'd had the best sex of her life with him.

NICOLA MARSH has always had a passion for writing and reading. As a youngster, she devoured books when she should have been sleeping, and later kept a diary whose content could be an epic in itself! These days, when she's not enjoying life with her husband and son in her home city of Melbourne, she's at her computer, creating the romances she loves, in her dream job. Visit Nicola's Web site at www.nicolamarsh.com for the latest news of her books.

OVERTIME IN THE BOSS'S BED

NICOLA MARSH

~ Seduction in the City ~

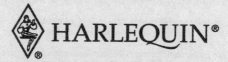

HARLEQUIN®

TORONTO • NEW YORK • LONDON
AMSTERDAM • PARIS • SYDNEY • HAMBURG
STOCKHOLM • ATHENS • TOKYO • MILAN • MADRID
PRAGUE • WARSAW • BUDAPEST • AUCKLAND

Recycling programs
for this product may
not exist in your area.

ISBN-13: 978-0-373-52771-7

OVERTIME IN THE BOSS'S BED

First North American Publication 2010.

Copyright © 2010 by Nicola Marsh.

This edition published by arrangement with Harlequin Books S.A.

For questions and comments about the quality of this book
please contact us at Customer_eCare@Harlequin.ca.

www.eHarlequin.com

Printed in U.S.A.

OVERTIME IN THE BOSS'S BED

This one's for my dancing buddy Jen.

Remember how we used to burn up the floor at
Bobby McGee's and the Geebung?
Fun memories…

CHAPTER ONE

THE BRONZE GOD WAS NAKED.

Gloriously, eye-poppingly naked, every muscle flexing and bunching and glistening as he carried a tray laden with cocktails and champagne flutes through the crowd.

'You can close your jaw now, before it hits the floor.'

Starr Merriday blinked once, twice, the spell broken as she tore her reluctant gaze away from the waiter and frowned at her best friend Kit.

'It's your fault. You brought me to this den of iniquity.'

Kit wiggled her eyebrows suggestively, her chuckle positively wicked. 'Yeah, and you're loving every minute of it.'

'It does have its benefits.'

Starr's gaze strayed to the ripped waiter again, lingered on his pecs, the light smattering of dark hair across his broad chest, dipped to his navel, the arrowing of hair beneath it...

'Jeez, what does a girl have to do to get a drink in this place?'

Kit smirked. 'Bit hot under the collar?'

'More like hot all over,' she muttered, thankful the waiters were clothed from the waist down, beyond thankful Kit had chosen one of her entrepreneurial mother's infamous cocktail parties for her farewell.

Nothing like a roomful of semi-naked guys to get a girl's mind off the fact she was jobless, homeless and penniless.

'Don't look now, but I think he's checking me out.'

Kit's subtle head-jerk towards Mr Pecs had Starr darting a quick glance in his direction, just in time to see him stumble, the tray skating on his palms like a penguin on ice, sloshing cocktails everywhere, the bulk of them landing on the guy next to him.

Sympathy warred with mirth as she watched the waiter try to mop up the mess, the guy in the suit waving him away with a frown.

The cocktail-wearing recipient looked out of place, suited and buttoned-up in a roomful of semi-naked guys, and she grinned as he fiddled with the knot of his tie, straightening it, aiming for cool, despite having several mojitos and a magnum of champagne dumped on his Armani duds.

'Yeah, he was definitely checking me out. Just one look and the guy does that. Back soon, hun. Off to mingle—find me a less clumsy one.'

Kit headed for the bar—and a tempting conglomeration of buffed waiters—while Starr found her gaze drawn back to the suit.

She'd been too busy ogling the waiters to notice the other guys in the room, but now she had... Slick guys in suits weren't her thing, but there was something about this guy. The way he stood, tall, proud, indomitable, despite a cocktail-dousing, his class obvious, his imperious gaze scanning the crowd...clashing with hers.

Startled, she dropped her gaze, surprised by the lick of heat lapping her skin after their momentary eye-lock.

The smart thing to do would be to quickstep out of here. But considering the shambles her life was at the moment, she hadn't done the smart thing in ages.

Curious to see if her inexplicable reaction to the stranger had been a result of a testosterone overdose from being in this room too long, she slowly raised her gaze to his. The moment of impact was just as cataclysmic as the first time.

He arched an eyebrow, his dark eyes filled with questions she had no hope of answering, the sardonic twist of his mouth tempting her to march right over there and set him straight.

She wasn't interested.

His lips curved in a decadent smile, shattering that particular delusion.

Damn, she was a sucker.

The only reason she'd come tonight was to avoid mulling. She'd already done the pity party earlier that week, complete with crashing cymbals, tooting horns and a banner that had read 'Fallen Starr', reminding her of the utter mess she now faced, courtesy of one lousy decision.

She'd fallen for the wrong guy.

Never again.

So what the hell was she doing, standing here, encouraging some serious eye contact flirtation with absolutely no intention of following through?

Sculling the rest of her drink, she headed for the glass-enclosed balcony fifty storeys above Sydney. Maybe some fresh air might give her a little perspective. Yeah, right, and a miracle might drop from the heavens too.

Leaving the jam-packed room, laden with expensive perfume and excessive testosterone, she stepped onto the balcony, grateful for its solitude, impressed by the view.

No doubt about it—Kit's mum knew how to throw top shindigs. Sydney came alive at night, shimmied and salsa-ed and samba-ed from dusk to dawn, and she loved it—loved every vibrant inch. As she watched a Manly ferry leave Circular Quay on a journey it made many times a day, the lights of the bustling city twinkling far beneath, the impact of leaving slammed into her hard, hurting despite the week she'd had to adjust.

Sydney was her past, Melbourne her future.

'Running away?'

The deep voice washed over her, and she shivered despite the balmy summer evening as *he* stepped in front of her—so much more striking up close, so much more appealing, so much more *everything*.

She couldn't see the colour of his eyes, or read their expression out here in the shadows, but there was no mistaking the amusement lacing his smoother-than-velvet voice.

He'd followed her out here, was trying to get a rise out of her, and while her first instinct was to tell him where to go, she swallowed it.

She'd never been one to wallow, and while her life

as she knew it had just been flushed down the toilet and discharged into Sydney Harbour, there was no time like the present to test her new male-immunity programme.

'Just needed some fresh air. What's your excuse?'

'Too many people back there—' he jerked his thumb towards the packed room '—and the only interesting ones are out here.'

'Smooth.'

'I like to think so.'

'Also terribly lame.'

He crooked his finger, and she inadvertently leaned forward.

'Care to help me improve my technique?'

'Nope. Not in the mood for meaningless small talk and pitiable one-liners.'

He laughed. 'How about a meaningful exchange?'

'Not interested, mister.'

She jabbed at his chest, realising her mistake a second too late as she connected with a hard wall of tempting male flesh.

His mouth twitched as she removed her finger *tout de suite,* the initial electricity zap from touching him fading into a residual tingle.

'Point taken.'

He didn't budge, didn't move a muscle even as she belatedly realised a big, strong, he-man like him would see her reluctance as a challenge.

'Doesn't mean I'm going to back down, though.'

She raised an eyebrow, surprised by his commanding tone. Who *was* this guy anyway?

'Look, unless you have a dream job in Melbourne's premier dance company to coerce me into listening to any more of your drivel, beat it.'

Her feistiness didn't deter him. He folded his arms, propped himself against the balcony railing, his expression intrigued.

'You need a job?'

'Oh, yeah.'

Desperately. Dance companies in Sydney were out, so she'd booked a ticket to Melbourne, ready to audition her little tap shoes off in order to find a job—any job—and start rebuilding her life.

'I've got a vacancy.'

She screwed up her nose, her withering glare doing little to discourage him if his confident grin was any indication.

'Let me guess. Cleaner? Cook? Shoe-shiner?'

'Close. I'm after a Girl Friday.'

'Too bad I'm a weekend kind of gal.'

He leaned closer, heart-stoppingly closer, and as she submerged the urge to bury her face in that broad chest she took a steadying breath, only to be bombarded with an intoxicating blend of fresh limes, tequila and strawberries. Fruity and tart, a heavenly cocktail mix, shaken and stirred, and served by one hell of a guy.

'You always this brash?'

'You always this forward with someone you don't know?'

'Easily rectified.'

He held out his hand, leaving her no option but to

take it, gritting her teeth against the insane surge of heat sizzling up her arm.

'Callum Cartwright. CEO of Cartwright Corporation. In desperate need of a temp PA 'til I find a long-term replacement.'

She slipped her hand from his, dropped it to her side, curled and uncurled her fingers several times to eradicate the residual tingling.

'Starr Merriday. Dancer, not PA.'

'Too bad.'

He slid a card from his top pocket, handed it to her.

'In case you change your mind.'

With an annoyed huff, she shook her head. 'You just don't give up, do you?'

'Not in my vocabulary.'

She toyed with the card, flipping it between her thumb and index finger, dying to glance at it but not wanting to give him the satisfaction.

'Let me guess. You're one of those demanding, controlling, determined bosses who won't take no for an answer.'

An odd expression she couldn't decipher creased his brow for a second before vanishing.

'You don't get to be the best by settling. For anything.'

Excitement rippled through her—whether from his drive, his power or his proximity, she had no idea.

'I'll keep that in mind.'

'Sure I can't tempt you?'

She could play it safe, give him a boring brush-off. But she was through playing it safe. Look where safe had got her for the last few years.

Uh-uh. Safe was for being the best at her job, staying loyal to one dance company for seven years, trusting her partner. And look where she'd landed anyway.

Forget safe.

'That depends.' She leaned into his personal space, her reeling senses on overload. 'What's on offer?'

This close, she could see his eyes were dark—deliciously dark and enigmatic—though she didn't need to be Sherlock Holmes to figure out the mystery behind them right now.

He was turned on: pupils dilated, eyes wide, pheromones creating a sensual cocoon around them.

The buzz she'd experienced when jabbing his chest had returned tenfold, multiplying and stultifying and defying her to take a risk.

'You don't want the job, so what *do* you want?'

She wanted to push the boundaries, to flirt, to feel feminine and desirable and wanted—all sadly lacking in her last relationship.

But was it worth inviting a potential one-night stand on her last night in Sydney?

For one drawn-out, exciting, tension-fraught moment, with Callum Cartwright staring into her eyes, she was sorely tempted.

CHAPTER TWO

COURTING a potential business partner was the only reason Callum had attended another boring cocktail party tonight.

He'd made the requisite circle of the room, shaken hands, slapped backs, and had been counting down the minutes deemed polite enough before leaving when that klutz of a waiter had bumped into him.

He'd been less than impressed—until he'd locked eyes with the gorgeous blonde on the other side of the room, and suddenly his drenched shirt hadn't mattered, the evening had not been so mundane.

He was a firm believer in following instincts. His gut reaction had made him millions in the financial arena, where Cartwright Corporation ruled.

So when she'd fled, he'd followed.

She'd verbally retreated. He'd verbally sparred.

And he'd been getting somewhere too. Her flashing eyes and lush mouth had been at odds with her defensive body language...until this.

Fishing his vibrating mobile phone out of his pocket, he glanced at the caller ID and begged off the luscious blonde, asking her to wait for him as he headed for the far side of the balcony.

He never turned off his mobile phone—the height of rudeness, as his last PA had kept reminding him. But then she didn't run a corporation and control billions of dollars. The money market never slept, and neither did he these days.

He hadn't slept in a long time—not since the fateful night that had catapulted him into this business in the first place.

And that was why he had to take this call.

Not because it would make or break Cartwright Corporation, but because it was from the one person who understood exactly what had happened that night, and was still dealing with it in his own way.

Taking a deep breath, he stabbed the answer button. 'Rhys, how's it going?'

'Not bad, bro. You?'

'Same old. Where are you?'

'Japan for a few more days, then I head for the States.'

'You coming home eventually?'

'We'll see.'

A resounding no, as usual. While he'd thrown himself into the family business after the accident, Rhys had fled. Studying interstate, escaping overseas once his degree came through, avoiding Melbourne and everything being a Cartwright entailed.

Callum envied him.

He'd been like that once, a lifetime ago, when he'd been carefree and selfish and irresponsible.

When he'd still had an older brother.

The Cartwright boys, people had called them, lumping them all in together. They'd been a team— before the accident, before Archie died, before their lives had been turned upside down.

'Where are you?'

'Sydney. Some boring cocktail party for work.'

Rhys paused, the faint static doing little to disguise the concern in his voice.

'Better than being alone tonight?'

Callum mumbled a noncommittal response, rammed his free hand into his pocket, and deliberately relaxed his tense shoulders.

He didn't want to discuss this.

He never wanted to discuss it.

Talking about what had happened this night fourteen years ago wouldn't change it. Nothing would.

'I'm hanging out with some mates tonight.'

'Good.'

Silence stretched, as it always did on their rare phone calls. They didn't have much to say to one another these days, what with most topics invariably leading to the past and what they'd done.

He glanced at his watch, cleared his throat. 'Do you need anything? Money?'

'I'm all right, but thanks.'

'Okay, then. Gotta go.'

'Cal?'

'Yeah?'

He heard the faintest hiss of breath before Rhys said, 'It wasn't your fault.'

Callum disconnected in a hurry, the gut-wrenching twist of sorrow deep in his gut telling him otherwise.

It *was* his fault—every shocking, mind-numbing moment of that night fourteen years ago.

He could forget most days, chase away his demons by submerging himself in business until the figures blurred before his eyes, but on nights like this it all came rushing back in an agonising avalanche of horrific memories.

Rubbing a weary hand across his eyes, he shoved the phone back in his pocket, turned, scanned the crowd for the blonde.

She'd vanished.

He wanted to pick up where they'd left off, to continue their flirtation. She'd be a firecracker, he could tell. All sass and mouth. Just the type of distraction he needed right now.

Tonight he wanted to forget.

Everything.

He'd thrown the job offer out there as a challenge, though a small part of him had hoped she'd take him up on it. He needed a fill-in PA desperately. The only temp agency he trusted had no one available for eight weeks and he was seriously floundering.

Even a beautiful dancer, with a smart mouth, a movie star name and a body built for ballroom rather than clerical, would be better than his current predicament.

He scanned the crowd, the entrance, finally spotting her beneath a towering indoor plant near the lobby.

He should leave, head back to his hotel, find solace in

a pricey single malt Scotch. Instead he found his feet veering towards her, and at that moment she glanced up, tossed her blonde hair and pinned him with a curious stare.

The impact of those large blue eyes slugged him all the way to his toes.

She glowed with vitality, from the tips of her silver-painted toenails to the top of her mussed, just-out-of-bed hair.

She wasn't his type—far from it. But there was something about her, something about her boldness, that reached to him on an instinctual level.

'Is it too much to hope you're waiting for me?'

'Way too much.'

'I asked you to wait around for me back there.'

Shrugging, she flicked a less-than-impressed stare his way. 'Guess I don't always do as I'm told—so sue me.'

Oh, yeah, she was a firecracker all right. Exactly what he needed tonight: hot, feisty, sassy, a world away from wallowing in memories he'd rather forget.

'Yet you're still here?'

She cocked her head to one side, studying him. 'I was waiting to say goodbye to a friend, but I think she's ditched me for one of those hunky waiters.'

'What? Those fake-tanned, muscle-bound Nean-derthals?'

Her glossed lips curved into a smile and he couldn't tear his gaze away.

She had the most beautiful mouth he'd ever seen: full lips, even white teeth, and a smile that could make a man forget where he was and why.

'Naked himbos not your thing?'

'Himbos?'

'Male equivalent of bimbo.'

She rolled her eyes, her tolerant expression reading *don't you know anything?* as he chuckled.

'Looks like she's a no-show.'

She pushed off from the monstrous terracotta pot where she'd propped herself, partially hidden amid the lush foliage of a palm, and it hit him all over again how utterly beguiling this woman was.

It had little to do with the sexily mussed blonde hair hanging halfway down her back, the wide luminous blue eyes or the saucy smile curving her lips, and more to do with the aura of vibrancy that shimmered and danced around her. Intriguing for a guy like him, who focussed on business all the time.

He'd never met anyone like her—only dated well-dressed, well-heeled, well-put-together socialites who played things cool.

Starr Merriday was hot, the antithesis of every woman he'd ever been with, and he couldn't walk away.

'Let me take you home. Make sure you get there safely.'

He'd expected an instant rebuttal and waited, captivated by her inherent beauty, her natural grace, her spunk.

He wanted to *demand* she let him drive her home, give him more time with her. His last PA had called it his God Complex—his need to control everything and everyone around him. He preferred to see it as staying on top of things. He was a guy used to being in charge and liked it that way.

'You want to take me home, huh?'

She cocked a hip, boldly provocative.

'That's what I said.'

She worried a gloriously full bottom lip for a moment, and he clamped down on the urge to do the same.

He wanted her.

Irrationally.

Madly.

Passionately.

With a brisk nod, she tucked her hand into his elbow.

'Fine. Have it your way.'

Gritting his teeth against the urge to grab her hand and make a run for the lifts leading to the hotel's exquisite rooms, he took a step forward, surprised when she didn't fall in beside him.

'Where to?'

'This way.'

He didn't trust her mischievous smile, the wicked sparkle in her eyes, and when she led him away from the monstrous glass entrance and towards the lifts, the rush of blood pounding in his ears signalled he was in way over his head with this one.

'You're staying here?'

She nodded, her smile widening. 'Just for tonight. My friends' shout for my last night in Sydney.'

'Where you headed?'

'Melbourne.'

'Great city.'

He should know. He'd taken it by storm years ago, had built his fortune there.

'You know I wasn't joking about that job offer, right?'

'I think we can find more fun things to talk about than my unemployed status.'

She stabbed at the lift button, raised her head to watch the numbers descend from ten to zero while he studied her.

He wanted her. Now. Wanted to lose himself in her, lose himself in the pleasure of hot, wild sex, lose focus of everything but her.

The doors pinged open. The lift's interior was a dazzling gold and chrome combination, with mirrors reflecting their images, showing a mixture of excitement and anticipation.

She stepped in, tugged on his hand. 'You coming?'

These days he always did the right thing, the cautious thing, the sensible, well-thought-out thing. But in that instant, with her eyes insolent and her lips curved into a brazen challenge, he did the thing he'd used to be famous for in his youth.

'Hell, yeah.'

Without releasing her hand, he stepped into the lift as she stabbed at the twenty-five button, the adrenalin rush of doing something out of character making his head spin faster than the lift's acceleration.

'You're awfully quiet.'

'Just thinking.'

'About?'

He pinned her with the glare that made most of his employees quiver.

'What it is about you that's so fascinating.'

She batted her eyelashes, her coquette's smile adorably tempting. 'I'll take that as a compliment.'

'You should.'

'So, have you figured me out yet?'

He trailed a fingertip down her cheek, tracing the soft curve.

'I'm getting there.'

His fingertip reached the end of the trail, lingered on her jaw, savouring the soft skin. 'You're unique.'

'And?'

'And I want to know more.'

The bell pinged again as the doors slid soundlessly open.

'I want to spend all night discovering more.'

He held his breath as she reached up, hooked a finger under his collar and tugged gently, bringing him tantalisingly close to her kissable lips.

'That can be arranged.'

CHAPTER THREE

STARR fumbled with the key card to her suite, sliding it through the slot three times before Callum placed his hand over hers.

'Let me.'

He tried the card again, the tiny button lit green, and she yanked on the handle, stumbled through the door. She was never this gauche, this flustered, but riding up in the elevator with this incredibly sexy man had been pure torture.

They'd barely touched, their hands simply brushing when she'd first punched in her floor, yet the tension between them had been indescribable.

Her skin prickled, her muscles clenched, and her pulse pounded in a rhythm she hadn't experienced for ages.

She'd been a one-man woman too long. A woman who'd been sadly neglected in the bedroom. A woman who wasn't terribly impressed with the supposed joys of sex.

Time to reawaken her flirty side.

As he reached out, his steady hand resting firmly in

the small of her back, burning a sizzling path straight through the thin silk of her dress, zapping her in places in desperate need of some serious zapping, she could barely restrain herself from launching at him.

'Come in. Make yourself at home.'

She silently cringed at her moronic, trite welcome, and the corners of his mouth curved upwards, creasing his right cheek with a delectable dimple.

'I intend to.'

Flinging her sparkly evening bag on the hall table, she trailed her hand along the shiny glass surface, rearranged the fronds of a floral arrangement, fiddled with the miniature alcohol bottles on top of the mini-bar, while he stood just inside the doorway, looking utterly cool and controlled and scrumptious.

Deliberately stilling her hands, she clasped them in front of her before realising how prim that looked, quickly releasing them and settling for propping them on the table behind her.

'I'm clueless as to the etiquette here. Do I offer you a drink? A chocolate bar? Me?'

His dimple deepened. 'The last, thanks.'

Her heart leaped, and she clenched the table so tight the mini-bar bottles rocked and rattled. One tumbled.

'Shaken or stirred?'

Laughing, he stalked towards her. Her pulse accelerated with each step. He stopped inches away from her personal space, his intentions clear in the dark depths of his eyes. The simmering heat sparked a response deep within her.

'Relax.'

He reached out, ran a fingertip down her bare arm, and she shivered in anticipation.

'Easy for you to say.'

'You're nervous?'

'A little.'

'Don't be.'

The trail of his fingertip ended at her hand and he captured it, intertwined his fingers with hers, giving her a much needed anchor in a suddenly stormy sea of passion.

His hand engulfed hers, strong, capable, and a lick of heat shot up her arm. She searched her scrambled brain for the right words—any words that would sound remotely sane and nothing like *ravish me now, I'm yours*.

'I can leave if you want.'

Cue the exit music. Cue the curtain call.

But not before they'd had a rousing performance.

Reaching out with her free hand, she bunched a fistful of his soft cotton shirt and tugged. Hard.

'I don't want you to go—'

He crushed his mouth to hers, snatching the rest of her words, the rest of her breath, in an explosion of heat and passion and driving need.

She clung to him, desperate to get closer, elated when he hauled her into his arms and backed her up against the nearest wall.

Wrapping her legs around him, she gasped at the bulge pressing against her core, her pelvis moving of its own volition, eager for more, demanding satisfaction.

'Oh, yeah,' she murmured, as he cupped her butt, moved back and forth, rubbing against her, teasing her, making her wild with wanting him.

He tore his mouth from hers, his passion-glazed stare mirroring hers.

'This is crazy.'

'Yeah, crazy…'

Resting his forehead on hers, he shook his head. 'I don't do impulsive stuff like this.'

'Me either.'

Sliding her hands up from his chest, to cradle his face and push it back until she could look him in the eye, she knew she couldn't stop this.

She didn't want to.

The old Starr had crashed to earth around the time she'd walked in on Sergio, in their apartment, in bed with another woman.

Time to say farewell to her old life. Time for the new Starr to rise and shine brightly. Starting with losing herself for one incredible night with a hot guy.

'What do you want to do?'

'This.'

She didn't second-guess her decision, didn't give it another thought as she drew his face back to hers and plastered her lips to his, arching her pelvis, locking her legs tighter around his waist and squeezing.

His low, guttural groan ripped the air as he deepened the kiss, ravaging her mouth, their tongues mating in a sensuous dance as old as the waltz.

Long, hot, moist French kisses went on for ever,

bringing her to the edge without him laying a finger anywhere near her throbbing core.

Tension tightened within her body, built, climbed, until she was boneless with desire. She clung to him as he left her mouth, his lips trailing downwards, nipping her erect nipples through the thin silk of her dress. His hands toyed with the edge of her panties beneath her bunched skirt.

Clamping her knees around his hips, she groaned, arched upwards—demanding more, demanding everything he had to give.

'If you keep making sounds like that, this isn't going to last long.'

'Fast is good,' she bit out as he nibbled her neck. She grabbed his hand from her butt and guided it between their bodies. 'Hard and fast.'

He tensed, every magnificent inch of him straining towards her. 'You sure?'

'Sure… Ooh…yeah…'

Holding on tight, he moved her from the wall to a nearby chair, rested her butt on the padded edge before leaning back to devour her with his hungry gaze.

'You're gorgeous,' he said, his husky tone bordering on reverent as he made quick work of the buttons holding her dress together, almost ripping it in his haste to get her naked.

She quivered with anticipation as he let out a long, low whistle, snapping the front clasp on her bra, pushing it aside before ducking his head to feast on her.

First the right breast, then the left. He licked and

suckled and laved until her head thrashed, her hips arched and her hands delved between them, eager to feel him inside her. Now.

'Wow.'

Her hand briefly encountered an erection, a very large erection, and then he pulled back.

'You want fast? I'm assuming not *that* fast?'

She laughed, amazed they were trading banter as if they'd known each other a lifetime.

Sex with Sergio had been lacklustre, had never given her the true intimacy she craved. Not that this mind-blowing foreplay with a guy she'd just met could be classed as intimate, but there was something about him that set her at ease, despite the fact she was almost naked in front of him.

Reaching up, she scraped her nails lightly down his chest.

'I want you. Now.'

'Decisive. I like that.'

He tugged her panties off, delved his fingers into her slick heat and pleasured her until she screamed his name. Twice.

'You're so hot,' he murmured, reaching into his back pocket, pulling a condom out of his wallet and sheathing himself before she'd even realised he'd ditched the pants.

Eyeing his impressive arousal, she said, 'So are you.'

His blistering stare never left hers as he slid into her, inch by exquisite inch, until he filled her, fulfilled her.

'Jeez…'

He braced himself over her, moved out a fraction,

back in, the delicious erotic friction sparking fire as her hips bucked, her insides clenched.

With a low moan he drove into her, again and again and again, harder, faster, his breathing ragged as her hands dug into his hips, urging him on.

This time her orgasm smashed into her with the force of a Sydney hailstorm and she arched upwards, her mouth slamming into his as he tensed and exploded in his climax.

His barely audible expletive echoed her thoughts, echoed what they'd just done.

She'd just had mind-blowing sex with a virtual stranger.

The best sex of her life.

A life which was out of control—which explained why she'd done this.

What she couldn't explain was the compulsion to do it all over again. Repeatedly.

Holding her close, he strummed her back and she closed her eyes, blindsided by the yearning to have him hold her and do this all night long.

'I should leave,' he said.

He should.

But she didn't want him to—didn't want to spend her last night in the only city she'd ever truly called home alone.

Leaning back, she cupped his cheek, looked him in the eye.

'Don't go.'

CHAPTER FOUR

STARR stared at the rumpled business card clutched in her hand and reread the address twice, before hoisting her backpack higher on her shoulder and pushing through the wrought-iron gate—the side gate, which would have been imposing in itself if it hadn't been positioned next to the hugest pair of intricately carved black iron gates she'd ever seen.

Some place, she thought, straining for a glimpse of the house as she strolled up the hedged garden path.

Sydney Harbour was lined with posh suburbs, with mega-million mansions vying for the best views and highest position, but from what she'd seen of the swanky Melbourne suburb of Toorak, it had its fair share of ritzy manors too.

She'd once dreamed of living in a place like this—around the time she'd scored the coveted lead dancer role at Bossa Nova. Ironic that now she might be working in one.

With her résumé and reputation she should have waltzed into a top dancing role in Melbourne. But

Sergio's vengeance knew no bounds, and the few doors she'd tentatively knocked on had been well and truly slammed in her face.

He'd been at fault, unable to keep his tights hiked up while getting it on with a fellow dancer, and she'd gladly left him—yet she was the bad guy in all of this?

Prima donna. She should have left him a long time ago—had chastised herself countless times since for sticking around so long for the convenience of having a great apartment within walking distance of work, a partner who understood the demands of being a dancer, and a guy she felt comfortable around.

Waste of time and money, considering she'd ended up paying the rent while he invested in a new dance company for *them*.

He'd promised her stardom and she'd let her ego get the better of her—had ended up almost broke when she'd walked out on the jerk.

No home, no money and no dance prospects explained why she was here.

Now all she had to do was go through with it.

Battling a surge of bitterness, she picked up her pace, rounded a corner and caught her first glimpse of the mansion.

Absolutely breathtaking.

She'd devoured Jane Austen novels as a kid, and standing in the shade of towering hedges, staring at the grandeur, she could have sworn she'd stepped into the pages of *Pride and Prejudice*.

The house—though how anything this size could

remotely be called a *house*—sprawled across a half-acre, its polished windows glittering in the morning sun, its pristine cream walls were blinding. Balconies dotted the upstairs rooms—elaborate twisted iron that accentuated the simplicity of the façade.

Classic, elegant, a grand old dame you couldn't help but admire. If the house was a dance, it would be an elegant waltz, gliding into the present from a bygone era, demanding recognition, admiration.

I could work here, she thought, wriggling her backpack into position before continuing down the path, hoping this interview went well.

She might not want this job but she needed it—desperately.

Admiring the shining marble of the front steps, she traipsed up to the front door, stabbed at the intercom button. A crackly voice filtered through the speaker, 'Around the back.'

Great. He wanted to make sure she knew her place right from the start. With a resigned huff, she followed the sandstone paved path to the rear.

If the front of the house had left her gob-smacked, the rear came a close second as she spied an Olympic-sized in-ground pool, a tennis court, a gazebo, and a terrace twice the size of the stage at the Sydney Opera House.

A lone figure sat a table on the terrace, phone glued to one ear, free hand hovering over a laptop keyboard.

He didn't glance up as she dumped her backpack and tripped up the steps. She waited for him to finish his call, forcing her feet to settle as she realised she was *en pointe,* a nervous reaction she'd had since she'd first started ballet at five years of age.

When he flung the mobile on the table and didn't glance up she cleared her throat, took several steps forward, hating how her knees wobbled a tad.

'Thanks for seeing me.'

Callum stood, turned towards her, his lips thin, compressed, at odds with her memory of how warm and soft and sensual they'd felt against hers.

'Good to see you again, Starr.'

His low, modulated tone reeked of formality, without a hint of what they'd shared.

'Though I must say I'm surprised you called.'

'Why? You gave me your business card, offered me a job.'

'One you scoffed at, if I recall.'

Hating his coolness, she squared her shoulders. 'Circumstances change. I'm interested in the position.'

His mouth quirked. 'Oh, really?'

Heck, she *had* stepped into a Jane Austen novel, complete with her very own Mr Darcy: pompous, arrogant, and way too gorgeous despite the urge to slap him upside the head.

'Is the job still available?'

'Very available.'

There it was—the first hint of something more than a job interview, a subtle reminder of what they'd shared laced through his smoother-than-caramel voice.

And in that instant it all came flooding back. Every

magical moment of their night together. Every cataclysmic, erotic detail.

How he'd stroked her to orgasm with his fingers, his tongue.

How he'd made her feel wanton and wicked and alive for the first time in for ever.

How he'd made love to her standing and sitting and in front of the bathroom mirror.

How she hadn't slept over the last week, replaying every moment of that life-altering night.

Technically, that wasn't right. Needing a job so badly she was now willing to work with the man she'd had an unforgettable one-night stand with rated right up there with life-altering.

Pressing her fingers to her eyes, she squeezed them shut in an attempt to block him out, blot out the enormity of all this. Spots danced and shimmered before them, and when she finally opened them, peeked between her fingers, her heart sank lower than the splits.

It was impossible to stand here and pretend to only view him as a prospective boss when she'd seen him naked.

'Shall we start the interview?'

His mouth kicked up into a semi-smile—a simple action that slammed straight into her, its impact just as brutal as she remembered.

'Yes, right. The interview.'

Inwardly cringing at her awkward response, she dropped her hands to her side, flexed her fingers, shook them out, mustered her best stage face.

'What do you want to know? My typing speed? PC skills? Microsoft literate? Multi-tasker?'

Heck, she was babbling, sounding more moronic by the second, while his expression remained impassive. His gaze focussed on her with frightening clarity, and she suddenly knew she'd been a fool to mistake this man for anything other than an imperturbable, composed businessman who'd let nothing stand in his way of getting what he wanted.

'I need you.'

'*You* need *me?*'

She laughed—a harsh, humourless cackle that startled a nearby magpie, which squawked in protest.

'By the looks of this place you don't *need* anybody. You're doing quite well on your own.'

His eyes narrowed, appraising, and she squared her shoulders and tossed her hair, glad she'd gone to the trouble of blow-drying it straight.

She needed to present a confident front—something she had no trouble with on the stage. Yet here, now, standing in front of this powerful man, she felt something deep inside quiver at the enormity of what she was doing: aiming to work for a guy who'd initiated her into the joys of sex. In a *big* way.

'I need a PA. Desperately.'

And she needed money. Desperately.

A win-win for them both.

If she could just forget the fact she'd had the best sex of her life with him.

She'd weighed her options and chosen to follow up

his job offer when she'd withdrawn twenty bucks from an ATM this morning and seen her bank balance slip to under a hundred dollars.

Time for further job-hunting wasn't a luxury she could afford, and his offer had niggled at the back of her mind—so tempting, so easy to chase up, so available…if only she could get past *this*. *Him*. The glorious memory of him naked that constantly flashed across her mind as she stood there.

But memories were worth nothing. The cost of starting a new life in a new city was way beyond her means if she didn't start working ASAP, and right now she'd be a fool to pass up an opportunity like this for the sake of her inner vixen, cringing with embarrassment at working for a guy she'd bedded.

'How soon could I start?'

He didn't blink, didn't move a muscle, his expression patient, as if dealing with a problem child.

'Immediately. You have all those skills you mentioned earlier?'

She refrained from rolling her eyes. Not good interview skills for a woman desperate for this job.

'I've temped before, in my early days as a dancer. Helped pay the rent.'

'Good.'

'Will I need book-keeping skills? Because—'

'Your duties may include some housekeeping, alongside the personal assistant stuff.'

'Housekeeping? But—'

'You'll find your remuneration more than fair.'

He ran roughshod over her, treating her like a subordinate, and she bristled, pulling herself up to her impressive five-ten. Pity it wasn't a patch on his six-four.

'Thanks. How much—?'

'And of course you'll be living in. The cottage will be yours, as part of your salary package, for as long as you work here.'

A cottage? All hers?

The next question died on her lips as she envisaged where she'd been staying for the last week: at a friend of Kit's, whose ramshackle inner city rental doubled as a local hangout for uni students without a place to sleep.

If she hadn't been haunted by memories of Callum she wouldn't have been able to sleep anyway—not with the crush of bodies littering the floor, the constant door-slamming at all hours, and the noisy bodily functions of uni students existing on a diet of stale pizza and baked beans.

She'd crashed there out of desperation and a lack of funds—counted on this job to get her out, depended on it for her first decent meal, something other than instant noodles and a recycled green teabag.

'You're welcome to check it out.'

Inwardly shuddering at the thought of any more tasteless noodles and weak tea, she said, 'Great.'

She followed him past the pool and a glass poolhouse, tucked behind immaculately trimmed hedges, and into a small clearing.

A small clearing that featured the most gorgeous little house she'd ever seen.

A cottage, just as he'd said, but what he'd failed to mention was its lemon rendered exterior trimmed in duck-egg blue, a criss-cross veranda housing a white wicker love-seat with striped cushions, and a border of petunias.

It was beyond cute, and the terracotta-tiled roof, reflecting the sun, seemed to shine directly into her eyes with some secret code that said *Live here!*

'Go on—take a look inside.'

He flung open the door and she exhaled, confronted by paradise. Her version of paradise: buttercup walls, their rich gold depths enhanced by honey floorboards, solid pine furniture, pot belly heater, monstrous suede sofas piled high with scattered cushions and a four-poster bed straight out of a fairytale.

This wasn't just any old ordinary cottage, no sirree. This place was a home—a place where she could start to rebuild her life, a place where she could instigate plans to get where she wanted to go.

'What do you think?'

'It's nice.'

Nice? *Nice?* The place was a flipping palace compared to the dumpster she'd been living in the last week.

'So you'll take the job?'

Ah…the job… The major catch in all this.

If she wanted to live here, she needed to work for His Lordship.

Whom she'd seen in all his naked glory.

Whom she'd kissed and caressed and kept up all night.

Oh, heck.

Folding her arms, she propped herself on the back of the sofa's headrest, ignoring how comfy it was.

'Isn't this at all awkward for you?'

There—she'd said it, flung it out there, trying to get a reaction out of him.

It didn't work. He didn't flinch, cringe, move a muscle. His expression was impassive.

'Why? Because we slept together?'

'You and I both know there was very little sleeping involved.'

It had been incredible—one of those once-in-a-lifetime nights that you stored away for wistful reminiscing in your old age.

The problem was the object of that fantasy night was standing right in front of her, looking way too cool in his designer duds, and the memory of the magic they'd shared was way too fresh.

'That night was a little crazy. I guess we both felt like company. Let's just leave it at that.'

She wanted to push the issue, wanted him to acknowledge there'd been far more between them than two people seeking company, but what was the point?

Nothing she could say or do would erase that night, and it sure wouldn't make working for him any easier.

Working for him.

She was seriously contemplating working for a guy she couldn't get out of her head, no matter how hard she tried?

'Fine, we'll leave it at that.'

It wasn't fine, but what choice did she have?

The old cliché 'beggars can't be choosers' sprang to

mind, and as she cast a longing look around the cosy cottage she knew what she had to do.

'I'll take the job.'

She stuck her hand out to cement her decision, but as his hand enclosed hers, firm, solid, way too warm, she wondered if she still had time to flee.

CHAPTER FIVE

CALLUM strode towards the house without looking back, annoyance lengthening his strides.

He'd miscalculated.

Made a *big* mistake.

Hiring Starr Merriday should have barely caused a blip in his busy schedule, but the moment he'd seen her standing on the veranda, wearing a black pencil skirt that accentuated her long legs and a tight ivory satin blouse, her hair silky-straight around her perfect heart-shaped face, he'd known.

He was in serious trouble.

The kind of trouble that couldn't be eradicated with a stab at the delete key. The kind of trouble that couldn't be fixed with money. The kind of trouble that would gnaw away at his subconscious until it drove him crazy.

It wasn't supposed to be like this.

He'd made that job offer on the spur of the moment—had flung it out as part of their sparring on an evening when he would have said and done practically anything to obliterate his memories.

He'd been disconcerted, on edge, considering the date—an anniversary he couldn't forget no matter how hard he threw himself into work, no matter how many millions he made.

Later, after Rhys' unsettling phone call, she'd helped him forget. Had blown his mind with hot, wild sex the likes of which he'd never had, and he'd lost himself in her rather than stew.

The way he'd seen it, the sex had guaranteed she'd never call him.

Yet she had. And when he'd answered the phone that morning, heard her voice as husky and sexy as he remembered, he'd agreed to see her.

For business purposes, of course. He was desperate, having had four temps walk out on him in the last twelve months, and he'd reached the end of his tether.

He'd tried every temp agency in Melbourne over the years, had been pushed to the limits every time. The temps they'd sent had covered the spectrum from too timid, too slow, too unmotivated, all the way to over-efficient, controlling, bossy types who'd tried to tell him how to run his business.

He refused to settle for anyone less than capable any more, and only worked with the best agency—the only one he trusted to deliver exactly what he needed. The one that couldn't send him anyone for eight weeks, apparently.

Then Starr had called, conjuring up an instant reminder of her feisty attitude, her dedication to her dancing in travelling to a new city to follow her dream, and the undeniable spark between them.

He'd had to hire her.

Desperation might have been his primary motivator, but he knew in his gut she'd be as driven to succeed in this job as in the rest of her life.

But working with the woman who for one unforgettable night had brought out an inner wildness he'd gone to great lengths to tame? Crazy.

He'd been determined her reappearance wouldn't rattle him. Yeah, *that* had worked.

Rattled? He was beyond rattled. Try unsettled, agitated, perturbed. Seriously perturbed on a level he didn't want to acknowledge, let alone recognise for what it was.

Seeing her again had resurrected the arguments he'd been having with himself since that night in Sydney: his voice of reason urging him to forget her while he'd contemplated looking her up, the impact she'd made on him versus concentrating on work, the one solid, dependable thing that had got him through the last fourteen years.

That was part of the problem too: his business had suffered because he couldn't stop thinking about her—something he wouldn't tolerate.

So he'd come to a decision: wait another week, then instigate steps to find her. If he saw her again, got this 'thing' for her out of his system, his equilibrium would be restored and everything back to status quo.

All nice in theory, and he should be thankful she'd approached *him,* but…he still burned for her. Seeing her in the flesh had dealt a total whammy to the cool, unemotional persona he'd spent half a lifetime developing.

And that didn't sit well with him. He didn't have time for emotions, let alone for a woman with a cheeky smile and twinkling eyes.

While he might have solved his PA dilemma, he had a feeling his troubles were only just beginning.

Starr waited until Callum had disappeared up the garden path before plopping onto a lovely squishy sofa and fishing her mobile out of her bag.

Hitting number two on her autodial—number one had been reserved for Sergio, and now stood satisfyingly empty—she waited for Kit to pick up.

'Hey, guys and dolls, you've called Kitty. Leave a message. I'll get back to you pronto. Toodles.'

After wrenching the phone from her ear and glaring at it, she shouted into Kit's answering machine.

'It's just after eleven so I know you're there. Pick up or else.'

She waited, counted to ten on her fingers, and had just raised her pinkie when a loud click signalled her nocturnal friend had finally surfaced for the day.

'Whaddayawant? Can't a girl get a little beauty sleep—?'

'Rise and shine, cupcake. Because I have news!'

Kit grunted in response, a loud rattle indicating she'd pulled her Roman blind down further.

'I found a job.'

Another grunt, followed by a muffled, 'What?' as Kit snuggled further under her duvet.

'It isn't a dancing position, but the cottage I get to

live in is sublime, and I'll keep job-hunting for something suitable, and—'

'Who you working for?'

'Callum Cartwright.'

'Hot.'

'Pardon?'

More duvet-ruffling before a much clearer and more
exasperated sigh filtered down the phone line. 'I said
hot. Apparently Callum Cartwright is a babe.'

'That's not the problem.'

'Problem?'

'He's the guy from the party.'

'What party—? Ooooh! *That* party. Working for a
sexy boss. Putting in some serious *overtime*. Lucky you.'

'Lucky? I have to act all professional and organised
and immune, when all I can think about is—'

'How hot he was in the sack?' Kit let rip with a big
fake sniffle. 'Boo-hoo.'

Starr smiled and tapped the phone.

'Hello? Looking for a little sympathy here. A little
*Ooh, you poor thing, Starr, having to work for a guy
you feel uncomfortable around.* Some of that wouldn't
go astray.'

Kit snorted. 'Give me a break. You don't need
sympathy—you need a wake-up call.'

By the sudden clarity of her friend's tone, Kit had sat
bolt upright and ditched the bedcovers completely.

'Listen up, girlfriend, for a bit of Kitty-Kat advice.
This guy rocked your world for a night. So he's your
boss now? Big deal. He's a temporary boss. You'll be

out of there as soon as you land a big gig, so why not make the most of your opportunity?'

Starr shook her head, her thumb hovering over the 'end call' button.

This was an interim job, a stop-gap, a fill-her-bank-account-with-something job while she did some serious searching for a prime dance role here in Melbourne.

Dance was her life, the only constant in her world— a world that had constantly changed and moved and evolved courtesy of her nomad parents, who'd hoe-downed, jigged and reeled their way across the country from the moment she was born.

She could depend on dance, could trust it to be there for her when no one and nothing else would. Her heart was poured into every performance, into every tango, every tarantella, every tambourin. Nothing was too great a sacrifice for her true love.

She'd forgone carbs and sugar for years to keep her body lean, had spent endless repetitive hours training until her back twinged, her hamstrings pinged and her eternally troubled feet ached. Had sat in audition queues for hours, nerves stretched tauter than a ballet shoe ribbon while checking out the competition.

It was worth it, every draining, exhilarating second, and the faster she accumulated a little security savings, the sooner she could ditch the PA duties and follow her dream.

Sure, she intended to give this interim job her all, but the fact she'd already slept with her boss made her beyond edgy.

'You're no help.'

Kit tsk-tsked. '*Au contraire,* Twinkletoes. I think I've merely voiced what you're already thinking. Am I right?'

Her muttered expletive had Kit chuckling.

'Go on, have a little fun. After what Sergio put you through, you deserve it.'

After what Sergio had put her through she deserved to spend a year in bed with Callum, uninterrupted.

'You heard he's set up his own dance company?'

'Yeah. Bastard.'

The company *she* was supposed to star in. Until he replaced her with a younger, lither model, both in and out of the bedroom.

'Like anyone's going to work for *him.*'

'Some of the Bossa Nova crew must've defected with him?'

Kit paused, cleared her throat, and Starr knew what was coming before her friend spoke.

'A few of the leads.'

'Aisha?'

'Uh-huh.'

Starr grabbed a nearby cushion and punched it hard.

'You shouldn't listen to gossip. I don't think she was with him when—'

'He was.'

She'd walked in on them, and while she'd wanted to kick both their bony asses at the time, when she'd calmed down she'd realised Sergio had done her a favour.

They'd been stagnant for a long time. She'd stuck with him out of familiarity more than any grand passion.

The kind of passion Callum had inspired during that one, incredible, unforgettable night, damn it.

'Anyway, enough about them. You need to focus. New job. Hot boss. Remember?'

She didn't need reminding. She had a feeling Callum would be crowding her head twenty-four-seven.

'Okay, you're right. I can do this.'

'Do *him*, don't you mean?'

Kit's wicked chuckle drew a reluctant smile.

'I'll keep you posted.'

'You do that. And, hun?'

'Yeah?'

'You need a break. So cut yourself some slack, enjoy the job, and live a little, okay?'

'Okay. Bye.'

'Toodles.'

After hanging up, Starr lay back with her hands behind her head and stared at the wooden beams criss-crossing the ceiling, Kit's friendly advice ringing in her ears.

Enjoy the job...live a little.

Unfortunately, she had a feeling the two weren't mutually exclusive.

CHAPTER SIX

'NEXT on the agenda is organising the business dinner for Friday night.'

Starr stared at Callum, hating the aloof control freak he'd morphed into.

Where was the suave, smooth guy who'd flirted with her that night in Sydney?

Where was the chivalrous, gallant guy who'd insisted he see her to her door?

Where was the hot, passionate guy who'd held her in his arms and made love to her all night long?

Vanished beneath a mountain of paperwork and memos and urgent e-mails, with his stuffy designer suit and starched business shirt covering a chest she remembered all too well.

'Is there a problem?'

She wrenched her gaze from his chest, noting with satisfaction the flicker of something other than aloofness in his deep, dark eyes.

'No.'

'Then concentrate.'

His snappish order dispelled any false idea he was thawing towards her. If anything, he'd been cold and abrupt to the point of rudeness since she'd started work.

He did have a problem with her, despite his little spiel about their night in Sydney meaning nothing.

Gripping her pen tighter, she doodled 'BAD MOVE' in bold capitals before blurting, 'Why did you hire me?'

His lips thinned before he fixed her with a no-nonsense glare.

'Because my work was backing up and you rang at the right time.'

'You know I won't be here long? That I'll be chasing up dance leads 'til I find something suitable?'

Steepling his fingers together, he leaned back in his director's chair, his expression that of a stern principal dealing with a recurrent problem child.

'I know everything about you.'

She blushed, hating how true that statement was.

He knew her erogenous zones, he knew her ticklish spots, he knew where she had a tattoo. A renewed surge of heat flushed her cheeks as she remembered how he'd traced the treble clef with his tongue, repeatedly.

'I'm under no illusions as to your length of stay. You'll be seeking employment as a dancer here in Melbourne. I expect that. In the meantime I'll continue searching for a permanent replacement.'

He sat forward abruptly, slammed his palm on the stack of documents in front of him.

'But for now I need you to get started on these.'

Pushing the teetering stack towards her, he barely

glanced in her direction, yet a telltale tic in the vicinity of his jaw alluded to an undercurrent he was desperately trying to hide behind work.

So the boss man wasn't quite as cool as he wanted her to believe.

She knew the feeling. Though his office was spacious, being confined in the same room as him, pretending they were just business colleagues, was taking its toll.

As hard as she tried to concentrate, every now and then her gaze would wander, honing in on one powerful, dedicated businessman.

She admired his drive, was grateful he'd hired her, but then her mind would wander along with her gaze, and she'd remember how driven he'd been that night in Sydney—a huge success in all areas of his life, including the bedroom.

Blinking, she cleared her throat. 'Where exactly would you like me to start?'

'Start at the top, work your way down.'

Oh-oh, her erotic memories had impeded her judgement, for she could have sworn she glimpsed a flicker of heat in his steady gaze, and her heart was doing the mambo as he leaned across the desk, so close, so temptingly close.

His lips quirked as he pushed the documents all the way across. 'From what you did with that stack of invoices earlier, this lot should be a breeze.'

Just like that her little fantasy that he was on the verge of flirting pirouetted out the window.

Of *course* he was talking about work, not alluding to that night in Sydney.

But there *had* been the twinkle in his eyes…

Gathering up the documents, she stood and headed for her desk, turning back at the last moment, catching him off guard, staring at her legs.

Yeah, she was right. He wasn't immune, and she'd be damned if she sat back and took all his 'this is work, I'm in control, that night never happened' crap.

'Just so you know—I don't play games.'

She expected him to feign indifference or ignorance. Instead, he crossed the room in one second flat to lean down and murmur in her ear, 'Neither do I,' before heading out through the door.

The moment he left she slumped into her chair, grabbed the nearest document and fanned her face rapidly.

While the air-conditioning kept the room at optimum temperature, working with Callum Cartwright did not.

Heat prickled her skin as she fanned faster, her cheeks burning. She couldn't afford to get this hot and bothered, couldn't let him affect her this way.

She needed this job, needed to stay focussed and on track so she could return to what she did best: dance.

Her hand picked up tempo, and the cooling breeze returned her temperature along with her common sense to normal.

There were a million and one perfectly logical, perfectly sane reasons why she couldn't get involved with her new boss.

Not mixing business with pleasure.

Her recent break-up.

The fact she wouldn't be around long.

And they were just for starters.

No, moving beyond a strictly platonic business relation-ship with her boss would be beyond stupid. And, while she might be many things, stupid wasn't one of them.

Flinging the document on top of the huge pile, she linked her hands, stretched overhead, enjoying the sat-isfying elongation of lats, trapezius, triceps, pushing muscles to their limit, only stopping at the twinge of pain that signalled she'd gone far enough.

Counting to a slow ten under her breath, she finally released her arms, shook them out.

Much better. Tension released, shoulders loose, ready to resume work.

Work would keep her focussed.

Work would keep her occupied.

Work would keep her from contemplating exactly how much fun it would be to replay that night in Sydney with her sexy boss despite the multitude of reasons not to.

Callum worked through dinner most evenings. It was the norm for him, burying his nose in work, and these days, with the economic downturn and investors both in Australia and abroad panicking, he needed to focus more than ever.

He'd used to think little of snatching a quick meal with his assistant as they wound up business for the day, getting a head start on tomorrow.

That had been before his assistant had sleek blonde hair hanging halfway down her back in a shiny curtain, a full bottom lip she constantly nibbled while concentrating, and a sensuously lithe body on constant display as she stretched every few minutes.

He'd been pushed into ballroom dancing as a kid starting high school—had been more interested in the girls wearing skimpy costumes than any burning desire to master the foxtrot or the cha-cha.

Surreptitiously watching Starr move reminded him of those old dance classes, the gracefulness of it all.

The simple action of her reaching for a pen became a fluid, elegant movement. When she switched from picking up the phone to jotting down notes it was a co-ordinated, smooth transition of elongated arms, flexible fingers and a slight stretch of her neck.

Her willowy body moved and shifted every few minutes, making the most innocuous tasks as riveting as watching an opening night performance of *Les Misérables,* his favourite theatre show.

He could have watched her for ever, but his pulse pounding a polka and the urge to choreograph them into more than a business relationship had him on edge.

He didn't do relationships.

Ever.

They'd moved past any potential awkwardness over their one night stand and he wanted to keep it that way. Getting physical again would only ruin the good working camaraderie they'd established in less than a day.

Nothing ever affected business. He wouldn't allow it. Yet without a good PA he'd been on the verge of floundering. He needed someone competent and she'd more than surprised him. Why botch that for the sake of reliving that one hot, unforgettable night in Sydney?

He watched her stand, reach for a file on the top of a cabinet, her toned right arm in perfect synchronicity with her left leg stretched behind, balanced on tiptoes.

She looked so poised, so controlled, so beautiful. He couldn't look away, trapped by the intense, overwhelming desire to cross the room, take her hand and spin her into his arms in one smooth move.

Frowning, he dropped his gaze, pinched the bridge of his nose.

Damn, this was a bad idea.

He'd had it all figured out: take her on as a stopgap measure so his business wouldn't suffer, ignore their night of passion in Sydney, stay on track.

Unlike his solid business plans, which always came to fruition through sheer doggedness and determination, this particular plan had hit a snag.

All the cool logic in the world meant nothing when confronted with Starr Merriday in all her glory.

Starr Merriday. Even her name sounded fun and frivolous and flirty. It fitted her perfectly, for that was exactly how she came across—no matter how hard she tried to handle the tasks he'd set her.

Not that she'd done a bad job—far from it. In fact, her diligence surprised him, as did her computer skills. She was nothing but competent and efficient and eager to learn.

He should have been happy he'd found someone at short notice; instead he silently cursed as his gaze drifted towards her for the hundredth time in the last half-hour.

Tearing a bite out of his usual cream cheese, smoked salmon and rocket sandwich, he tried to focus on the figures in front of him, but the numbers on the spreadsheet held little interest in comparison to surreptitiously watching a beautiful woman tapping industriously at a computer.

'If you keep staring at me like that I won't be responsible for typing a load of gobbledy-gook on this report.'

Sprung.

He'd bluff his way out of it, even though he was desperate to rein in the uncontrollable urge to sweep the work off the table, ditch dinner and feast on her.

'Who said I'm staring?'

With a defiant toss of her hair, she pushed away the keyboard, linked her hands and stretched.

And his mouth went dry.

Her blouse pulled taut against her breasts, taunting him, teasing the edges of his memory.

Not that it needed much prompting.

He could remember every luscious curve of her toned body: the smooth skin, the tempting indentations, the sensitivity of the hollows behind her knees, her elbows, the underside of her breasts, that wicked little musical tattoo on the upper inside of her right thigh...

'What's up?'

He snapped to attention, blinked to dispel the erotic fog clouding his judgement. Hell, he'd never get any work done at this rate, and it was only her first day.

'You're distracting me.'

She quirked an eyebrow, a smug smile playing about her glorious mouth.

'I'll take that as a compliment.'

He frowned, pointed at the keyboard. 'I meant your infernal clattering.'

He only just caught her muttered, 'Liar.'

Pushing away from the table, he headed for the back door. 'I'm going for a swim.'

'What about work?'

'You know what you have to do.'

'So I'm finished for the day once I'm done here?'

He nodded, hating how ungrateful he sounded, all because he couldn't ignore his raging libido.

'Thanks. Good job today.'

'My pleasure.'

He bit back a groan as her tongue darted out to moisten her bottom lip, his gaze riveted to it, his mind lingering on her last word.

Pleasure.

Raunchy, raw, steamy pleasure.

It was all he could think about with this woman, all he could fantasise about over and over and over...

Hating feeling this out of control—been there, done that, suffered the consequences every day of his life since—he wrenched open the door, grateful for the slap of cold air.

'We start at eight tomorrow morning.'

'I'll be here.'

The soft tinkle of her knowing laughter chased him out of the door.

* * *

Starr had never been a glutton for punishment.

When things weren't working out in her life, she cut and run.

She'd done it as a kid when she'd run away from her parents, who'd moved for the hundredth time, chasing their own dreams and ignoring hers.

She'd done it as a teenager when her attempt at leaving showbiz behind hadn't worked and she'd enrolled in a business course, only to leave two years later when she hadn't been able to ignore the lure of the dance studio.

And she'd done it recently, cutting her losses with Sergio and starting afresh in Melbourne.

So why was she punishing herself like this?

Hiding out in the shrubbery between the cottage and the pool, watching Callum cut through the water like a shark with the scent of prey.

This was definitely punishment—spying on something she couldn't have, something deliciously tempting that had tortured her all day.

She knew getting involved with him was wrong—had rehashed the arguments against it in her head several times over the last few hours while she'd been the model diligent PA and he'd pretended not to stare at her.

Considering she was currently wedged in a bush, with twigs poking her butt and pollen tickling her nose, she guessed she hadn't listened too hard to the reasons why she needed to keep her distance from this guy unless it was during business hours.

She might be desperate for money and a place to live but this was crazy. She needed to start making the rounds of dance companies again, dropping off résumés, muscling in on auditions.

She needed to get out of here.

With a shake of her head, she shuffled backwards out of the bushes, freezing when she heard a terrifying sound halfway between a growl, a snort and heavy breathing.

'Damn it,' she muttered, unable to see much in the deepening darkness, cursing Callum and his undeniable attractiveness that she had to end her day stuck in a bush perving on him rather than kicking back in the cottage relaxing in a heavenly bubble bath.

The sound stopped and she inched backwards, leaping in fright when it happened again, much louder and much closer this time. Casting a quick look over her shoulder, she screamed and scrabbled forward as two huge luminous eyes followed her every move.

'What the—?'

Spitting leaves out of her mouth, she glanced up to find Callum towering over her, deliciously wet. His glower would have been intimidating if not for all that glistening naked chest.

'What the hell are you doing down there?'

'Thanks for asking if I'm okay,' she said dryly, darting a quick glance back at the bush, wondering if she'd be better off taking her chances with the scary mystery critter than divulging the truth of what she'd been doing.

The corners of his mouth twitched as he held out his hand.

'Are you all right?'

'Apart from a serious case of dented pride, I'm fine.'

She took his hand, allowed him to pull her up.

Whoa! Naked alert! The words flashed across her brain.

But, just as she'd done a week earlier, she ignored it and placed her other hand against his glorious chest on the pretext of steadying herself.

Evening sounds of chirping crickets and settling birds faded to nothing, until all she could hear was the thudding of her heart, pounding loud and proud in her eardrums, in perfect sync with his.

Time slowed as she watched droplets of water trickle down his chest, riding the bumps of his defined abs before dripping lower into tempting oblivion.

He was the sensible one. He should step away.

Instead, when she tore her hungry gaze from his chest and met his there was no clash of wills, merely her raging need reflected in his hungry eyes.

'You make me crazy,' he muttered, a second before dragging her into his arms and crushing his mouth to hers in an explosive kiss that defied logic and sent her good intentions to focus on getting out of here clear into the night sky.

She didn't think, didn't rationalise, didn't feel anything beyond the cataclysmic explosion of passion rushing through her body, turning her weak with need.

Her hands skated across his chest, savouring every inch of deliciously hard, exposed muscle, her fingertips discovering his sensitive spots all over again, exploring by memory.

He groaned, the erotic sound torn from deep within, and without a second thought she jumped into his arms and wrapped her legs around his waist, bringing her core into exquisite contact with his arousal.

If the first explosive contact of their lips had wreaked havoc, it had nothing on the friction between their bodies, wet skin to thin cotton, rubbing and writhing and driving her wild.

He broke the kiss, nibbling her neck just the way she liked it, remembering every sensitive spot and discovering new ones as he trailed lower…and lower…

Her head fell back, blinding need ripping through her as she stared up into the sky, her body on sensory overload, craving his masterful touch. At the first brush of his lips against her breast she moaned, arched towards him, wishing this delicious madness could continue for ever.

Like most good things in her life it didn't. He stopped, raised his head, his expression shuttered as cold rushed between them, pebbling her damp skin where he'd been pressed against her.

'We can't do this.'

She could have cried in frustration as he untangled her hands from behind his neck, supported her butt as she uncrossed her legs from his waist, and set her down gently.

Of course they couldn't do this. She'd spent an entire afternoon mentally reciting the very same thing.

But acknowledging and accepting every logical reason why they couldn't do this didn't make it any easier to ignore the sizzle still zapping between them.

He frowned, shook his head, and she knew what he'd say before he opened his mouth.

'This can't happen. We work together.'

'Might've been a problem, but irrelevant considering we've already slept together. Kinda makes the whole harassment thing null and void.'

'That's not the problem.'

'Then what is?'

She tilted her chin up, curious to see what else he'd pull out of his bag of one hundred and one logical reasons not to get involved.

Probably nothing she hadn't already told herself, but the fact they'd both just lost control after a tense afternoon made her wonder.

What could he say to really douse this fire kindling between them?

'I don't have time for this.'

'No time for a little fun?' With a shake of her head, she tsk-tsked. 'That's not true and you know it. You date, right?'

A frown slashed his brow, while that telltale tic in his jaw flickered. She'd bet he used that narrow-eyed glare to good effect when intimidating others. It had little effect on her.

'Or do you just have meaningless sex with women before discarding them?'

He muttered a curse, clamped his lips shut.

Okay, so that last comment had been unfair, as she knew nothing about his personal life, but she wanted to goad a reaction out of him, wanted him to acknowledge that they couldn't ignore this explosive attraction between them even if they couldn't do anything about it.

'With you working here, staying in the cottage, it's too—'

'Close for comfort?'

Unable to resist touching him, she skimmed the dimple in his right cheek, the slight dent in his chin, her fingertip trailing downwards, lingering on the dip between his collarbones, enjoying the flare of heat in his eyes, the hiss of pleasure.

'I was going to say too complicated.'

'And you don't do complicated, right?'

Snap. Neither did she. She'd done complicated for the last few years; it was highly overrated.

Here was a guy who could give her what she wanted, could awaken her femininity, could teach her about pleasures she'd only dreamed about. He'd made a good start in Sydney, had shown her how good sex could be—yet another department in which Sergio had let her down—but she couldn't go there.

He was right. Anything other than business between them would be way too complicated.

She'd hustled her way out of one disastrous relationship—why jitterbug into another potential minefield?

He stepped back, his eyes wary, his expression grim.

'Let's just forget this ever happened.'

She nodded, relieved yet disappointed. 'A slight aberration…a blip on the radar.'

He held her gaze for a moment longer before turning away, but not before she heard his muttered, 'Some blip…' as he strode away as if he couldn't get away from her quick enough.

CHAPTER SEVEN

AS DAWN broke over Melbourne, scattering mauve and gold fragments across his desk, Callum yawned, stretched, swiped a tired hand over his eyes.

He hadn't pulled an all-nighter in a while, and his back protested as he stood, twisted, worked out the kinks.

Bracing himself against the windowsill, he stared out at the lightening sky.

How many dawns had he seen following the accident? Too many to count. Work was the only thing that kept him sane, kept the raw, relentless guilt from tearing him apart.

And to think he'd once embraced the dawn as he regularly stumbled in at five a.m. after yet another party, another celebration, another night out, high on life.

Nothing had held him back; he'd been free to do what he liked when he liked.

Until the night he'd gone too far.

And Archie had died.

Because of him.

Closing his eyes, he remembered another time, another life, another man he tried to emulate because of what he'd done, because it was the only way he knew how to make amends.

Pressing his fingertips into his eyeballs, he welcomed the pinch of pain before turning away from the window, taking a seat at his desk, casting an eye at his electronic diary for the day.

Back-to-back meetings—no room for anything other than business.

Another reason he'd pulled this all-nighter. To refocus on business, to banish the memory of Starr and that disastrous poolside kiss—a kiss he'd tried to forget, a kiss he'd relegated to the back of his mind by throwing himself into work, chairing a whirlwind of meetings, all interstate.

It hadn't worked.

He couldn't forget, no matter how hard he tried—couldn't forget how wild and out of control she made him feel despite his intentions to keep things between them purely business while she worked for him.

And that was what irked the most.

Not the fact he'd come to his senses too late, not the fact he'd been so befuddled he'd almost taken her on the spot, but the fact he'd lost total control to the point where he would have gladly had a repeat of that amazing night in Sydney.

He liked everything orderly and organised, rational and logical and in place. He thrived on organisation, on responsibility, and he'd be damned if he let some flirty enchantress turn his world upside down.

But what if she already had?

Pushing away from his desk in disgust, he grabbed

a mineral water out of the fridge, gulped it down, needing to chill out.

Sadly, while he was thinking about Starr, he knew he'd need all the ice in Antarctica to cool off.

Starr sipped the last of her strawberry smoothie, eager to duck into the office to ensure everything was set for Callum's return today before going for a quick walk before work.

She was stiff and grumpy from lack of exercise, her muscles protesting at the lack of a workout, and the last thing she needed was to take her frustrations out on the boss man's first day back.

He'd vanished the morning after their poolside kiss, citing meetings interstate and leaving her with a long list of tasks. She'd followed his instructions to the last meticulous detail, determined to prove she could do the job despite what had happened.

While *he'd* had the common sense flash during that kiss, she'd had seven long days to agree with him.

Sure, they had a...*thing* between them, but ignoring it shouldn't be a problem as long as they both concentrated on work.

Despite her doubts at the start about working for him after their one-night stand, she was nothing if not realistic, and that spontaneous kiss must have been a remnant of leftover attraction. Just one of those things. Unavoidable. Good to get out of the way—move on.

She loved to take chances, loved to jump into situations feet first, reserving thinking for later.

Not this time. This time she had to pretend the best sex of her life had never happened, focus on work for however long she stuck around, and ensure she had finances to fall back on.

'Good morning.'

She jumped as she stepped into the office, her heart leaping in recognition of that smooth tone.

'You're up early.'

As she turned and laid eyes on Callum—his pale blue business shirt rolled up at the sleeves, the top few buttons undone, tie-less—not only did her heart leap, it did a complete gymnastic routine of non-stop backflips any Olympian would have been proud of.

He was breathtaking. From the fabulous fit of his custom-made shirt to his highly polished Italian leather dress shoes and every inch in between.

Sergio had been handsome in a showy, flashy kind of way, but the understated sexy elegance Callum brought to a room just by being in it took her breath away.

'I got in late last night.'

'And you've been here since?'

'Uh-huh, loads to catch up on.'

As she'd expected, he'd retreated behind a wall of indifference after his week away, pretending that kiss had never happened.

'You'll find everything in order.'

'Good.'

His intent stare raised goosebumps and she had the feeling he was looking right through her.

She shuffled her feet, uneasy under his scrutiny,

wishing she could read his mind. She wanted to know what he was thinking, what he really felt about the undeniable attraction simmering between them—a constant reminder of that one, incredible night.

'I'm going to take a shower.'

He ran a hand through his hair, mussed it, and as he crossed the room towards her she saw the telltale dark circles under his eyes, the fatigue lining his mouth.

What drove this man to work like the devil? To pull an all-nighter his first night back home after a week of business meetings?

She'd been driven to succeed in her field, but never had she pushed herself like this.

'I'll see you back here shortly.'

'I'm going for a walk first.'

His eyebrows shot up, as if she'd announced she was planning to hula down Bourke Street.

'I don't start 'til eight, remember? Unless you want me for something urgent?'

Instant heat flared to life in his eyes, before he blinked, damped it.

'It can wait.'

His tone, brisk and businesslike, grated. Didn't anything ever rattle him?

'Fine. I'll see you later.'

She whirled away, annoyed at him, angry at herself for still wanting him despite her week of telling herself it couldn't happen. His hand snuck out and landed on her shoulder, halting her, gently spinning her around.

'What's wrong?'

Compressing her lips, she shook her head.

'You don't want to know.'

'Maybe I do.'

Her heart stilled as he leaned towards her, a tantalising waft of some expensive citrus aftershave washing over her, tempting her to merengue her way into his arms in two seconds flat.

The tense silence between them grew. Her skin was tingling with expectation, her breath choppy as her heart skipped to a mambo beat.

Anticipation. Nothing like it. She was addicted to it—loved the expectant buzz before she first stepped on stage, the rush of adrenalin as she took her first leap in a new dance routine.

Then, like now, she stood on the precipice of something great, something exciting, something to set her pulse pounding and send her body into sensation overload.

'I don't want anything affecting your work today. We've got loads to do.' He dropped his hand, stepped away. 'So whatever's wrong, tell me.'

Work. Of course. As if he cared about anything else—as if he gave a hoot about her.

Mentally calling herself every name under the sun for believing he was half as attracted to her as she was to him, she folded her arms, refrained from pouting—just.

'I miss my workouts, my dance practice. It's making me edgy.'

His probing gaze lingered on her for several long moments before he pointed down the corridor.

'The ballroom's that way. Feel free to use it.'

'Really?'

'Whatever it takes to get you focussed on the job.'

'Thanks.'

She should be ecstatic. She had a good job with a dependable income, a fabulous place to live, and now somewhere she could get back into shape before restarting her rounds of the local dance companies.

Things were looking up.

So why couldn't she shake her foul mood as she raised her hand in a wave and headed to the cottage to change?

Starr huffed into the ballroom.

She should be grateful Callum had allowed her access to this incredible space. Instead, she flung her towel and water bottle into a corner and cranked up the music on her iPod, needing to vent some of her anger through dance.

It had worked as a kid when she'd danced off years of resentment at her parents, it had worked after Sergio, and it sure better work now or she'd explode.

Maybe it was hormones? Maybe it was pique that Callum could pretend nothing had ever happened between them? Maybe she just needed to stretch and leap and fling herself around after being cooped up for a week? But, whatever the reason, she needed to obliterate her thoughts with what she knew best: dance.

The soft, ethereal beat of her warm-up music filtered through her ears, softening her muscles, making her nerve endings tingle with the familiar urge to move.

She stretched her neglected muscles: lengthening hamstrings, quadriceps, calves, enjoying the slight tug of pain indicating she'd never gone this long without working out.

Flopping forward, she swung side to side, shook her arms out, and as she straightened took several deep breaths and reached heavenward. The last of her anger disappeared on her fifth exhale.

Oh, yeah, this was exactly what she needed.

The music filled her. Filled her body, her senses, infusing her with peace she never found anywhere but in dance.

It was the reason she'd taken it up in the first place— a lonely five-year-old waiting on the front steps of the school for the umpteenth time, waiting for parents who either forgot her or didn't care or had more important things to do.

The school music teacher had found her that day, taken her into the hall to wait, and as she'd watched a group of girls shimmy their way between tap and jazz and ballet she'd been entranced.

When her mum had eventually turned up, an hour later, she'd begged to join the group, and Gladys had been only too happy to foist her off for another hour a day.

She'd loved the music, loved the graceful movement, loved the clothes. And for the first time in her life she'd belonged.

Though it had been more than that; for those all too brief hours at dance class she'd felt secure, and no matter how many cities her folks had dragged her to, how many schools she'd attended, she'd always felt safest when dancing.

Warm-up done, the next song on her playlist kicked in—her favourite R&B singer, who never failed to make her feel soulful and sexy.

She allowed the beat to take her, feet moving in time, shoulders loose, eyes closed, and in that moment she released all the frustration of the last few weeks: Sergio, Sydney, Callum...

Callum most of all. For being so damn responsible, too darn gorgeous, and way too work-oriented for his own good.

He needed to lighten up, to have a little fun. He'd been so buttoned-up this morning, so stern, so foreboding.

What would it take to get through to a guy like him? To break down the barriers he'd erected?

The music picked up tempo, and as she swung into a few jazz moves, comforted by the familiarity of doing what she did best, she knew getting the sexy CEO to relax was high on her agenda.

He shouldn't be doing this.

Watching her.

But Callum couldn't resist the lure of seeing Starr move and sway and gyrate to a beat only she could hear.

He watched her spin with perfect precision, glide and leap across the floor like a gazelle, wiggle her butt and gyrate her hips until all the blood from his head drained south.

Oblivious to her audience, she high-kicked and hip-hopped and stomped her way across the ballroom before slowing, her frantic whirlwind of movement becoming softer, more erotic.

Breathtaking.

His lungs seized with the effort of not dragging in great gulps of air to ease the tightness in his chest. He was scared of breaking the spell.

Crazy, as she couldn't hear him with the iPod earphones, but there was something so fragile about this moment, something so special, that he didn't want to risk it.

This was akin to spying on her private time, but he was drawn to her no matter how much he wanted to keep his distance.

Her feet picked up tempo and she raised her arms, her workout top pulling taut across her breasts and revealing a tantalising sliver of belly.

His groin ached, and he clamped down on the urge to march in there, haul her into his arms and dance body to body until they were slick with sweat, hot and frantic, desperate for each other.

He backed away, needing to escape before he did something irreversible.

Her eyes snapped open at that instant, fixed on the door, and she stumbled mid-step, her arms falling to her sides as she yanked out the earphones.

'Did you want me for something?'

Hell, yes.

He wanted her in his bed, in his shower, in his

Jacuzzi, in every damn room of his house, over and over and over again.

The memory of her body, her kisses, her caresses, were burned into the hard drive of his brain, no matter how many times he hit the delete key.

'No, keep going. Sorry to interrupt.'

'It's okay.'

They stood there, a yawning expanse of polished parquetry separating them, their wary reflections staring back at them from Viennese mirrors, neither making a move.

He never lost control, never lost sight of his responsibilities, but at that moment, with Starr staring at him with a beguiling mix of open curiosity and hidden desire, a sheen of perspiration adding a gleam to her skin and a body made for dancing and sin, he almost lost it.

'I've got work to do.'

He hated how abrupt he sounded—hated the hurt in her eyes more.

'I guess we both do.'

She turned away, but not before he'd seen her confusion.

She was confused?

That made two of them.

Ignoring the urge to barge into the ballroom, sweep her over his shoulder and lug her to his room, where they'd hole up for a week, he headed for the study.

Work would keep him focussed, centred, as it always did when his world tilted crazily out of control.

It had worked once before.

It sure as hell better do the job now.

CHAPTER EIGHT

STARR slipped off her killer heels as she exited the back door, wishing she could wear ballet flats to work, wiggling her toes in relief before heading down the path leading to the cottage.

If the gardens were impressive during daylight, they took on a new dimension in the moonlight. The pool sparkled with strategically placed lights, turning the water a translucent aquamarine, the grass took on the properties of emerald velvet, and the lights embedded in both sides of the pathway created a welcoming guide to home.

Home.

Something she'd always yearned for—something she'd prayed for as a child, beseeching Santa and the Easter Bunny and the Tooth Fairy and anyone else who would listen to her pleas.

But the people she'd needed to listen the most—her parents—had never paid heed. They'd continued on their merry way, skipping from city to city, chasing the next audition, the next big break. They'd dragged her all over Australia, venturing as far as London once to star in a pantomime, never caring that their only child wanted the one thing they couldn't give her: security.

A home. A real home, complete with knick-knacks and stacks of magazines and the general clutter people accumulated after living in one place for more than six months.

Instead she'd lived out of a suitcase, trying to share her parents' enthusiasm for each new place they settled, failing dismally when they picked up and moved again when the mood took them.

Foolishly, she'd thought she'd found that home with Sergio—had loved buying cookbooks and tapas platters and the magazines she'd happily stacked in a corner of their lounge room.

That dream had disappeared too—yet leaving him hadn't been as traumatic as leaving the home she'd created for them.

Now she'd found her version of idyllic, and as she tripped up the steps of the cottage, unlocked the door and let herself in, she mentally slapped herself for falling in love with a place in a week—especially a place she'd have no option but to leave.

With a heavy sigh she closed her eyes, leaned against the door, willing the cottage to morph into an ugly, cold abode.

She opened them and there it was, still as warm and cosy and utterly appealing as it had been the first moment she'd set foot in here.

This was a home, all golden-hued and warm and inviting. She'd never felt so comfortable, so secure, in a place she'd only just moved in to. But she couldn't get too cosy.

She needed to find a job in her own field, find a place to live, and while staying in the cottage was bliss, spending every waking moment in Callum's company was sheer torture.

Today had been hell.

Her early-morning workout should have relaxed her, eased some of her tension. Instead, being cooped up in Callum's office all day, having him bark orders and snap on the phone and look over her shoulder, had had her walking a fine line between quitting and sticking it out.

She needed this job. The only reason she'd gritted her teeth and smiled and acted as if she didn't have a care in the world as she'd completed every task he'd set her.

In all honesty she'd had worse bosses. Divas who'd pushed her, harangued her, made her stand at the barre and stretch until she'd thought her muscles would snap. International professionals who'd had their leotards in a twist while screaming at the chorines to stay in line, can-can higher, kazatsky lower.

She'd sweated litres and bitten back tears through a torturously long flamenco session, torn her Achilles' tendon during a carioca-criolla-mambo marathon, and fainted after an all-day session with a Polish choreographer who'd made her repeat the mazurka and polonaise until her arches cramped and her toes bled.

Compared to those control freaks she could handle working with Callum without getting her tutu in a knot.

Her glance fell on a tiny jade elephant perched on the

mantelpiece, its trunk jauntily up—signalling good luck, apparently.

It wasn't the only elephant in the room. The other one was right there with them every second of the day, whether they wanted to acknowledge it or not.

Here she was, holed up in the cottage, while the sexist man she'd ever met was probably slipping between satin sheets gloriously naked. What she wouldn't give to march back over to the house and demand they pick up where they'd left off with that poolside kiss.

But they'd drawn the line, wouldn't cross it again. Besides, getting physical with Callum a second time around would change their relationship, no matter how clear the rules, and she'd never been one of those girls able to compartmentalise her life.

When she got involved with a guy it was heart and soul, and handing her wary heart to a man like Callum would be like dancing *en pointe* with a broken toe: absolutely agonising.

He didn't do involvement, he'd made that clear, and while she agreed on principle, she knew the practice would be much harder.

Over the last week she'd toyed with the idea of a transient, light-hearted, no-strings-attached fling before slapping the idea down. There was no denying the itty-bitty twinge of hope in her heart that having fun with Callum might lead to more.

She liked being in a relationship, liked the intimacy, the hand-holding, the shared jokes. She loved snuggling up to a man last thing at night, waking in the crook of his arm first thing in the morning, and she really, really loved what happened in between.

It didn't take a genius to figure out she had security issues, that she needed a relationship to feel safe. It was why she'd stuck it out with Sergio so long, despite her gut instinct screaming that they weren't as close as she liked and never would be.

He'd suited her: same career, same circle of friends, same goals. But they'd started drifting apart after the first year. She'd glossed over it, throwing herself into making their apartment a home, content to pretend she had a great relationship when in fact it was mediocre.

And, while she'd wanted to chop off his philandering head when she'd walked in on him and his floozy in their bed, a small part of her had been glad he'd taken the decision out of her hands, leaving her no option but to leave.

Having a fling with Callum would be cathartic, would go a long way to cementing her new goal to have fun without the encumbrances of a relationship. But there was no denying her inner voice that made a mockery of her new pledge, discounting the fact they'd both agreed not to go there.

Muttering a few choice curses under her breath, she changed into her nightie, too tired to take the bath she'd hoped for, and slipped under the covers. She adored this bed—felt like a princess every time she slept under the filmy gauze draped from the top of the four posts.

The distant rumble of thunder grew closer as she

closed her eyes, hoping the storm passed quickly. She hated thunderstorms, courtesy of several doozies she'd faced as a kid in Queensland.

She'd never forget hiding crouched in a cupboard, hands over her ears, tears streaming down her cheeks, as howling winds rattled the windows and lightning lit up the darkness of their mobile home.

She'd been alone, of course. Her parents had been out for the evening, schmoozing some producer in the hope of a new role. How old had she been? Eight? Nine? Ironic that people needed a licence to drive a car but any fool could have a kid.

Her eyes flew open at a loud crack of thunder and she slipped further under the covers, wrapping her arms around herself in a comforting hug.

Okay, this was silly.

She'd lived through loads of thunderstorms, whether they frightened the bejeebies out of her or not, and this would be just another one.

Forcing herself to relax, she sat up, reached for the glass of water on the bedside table and took several sips.

A streak of lightning lit the sky, illuminated the room, and she tensed, bracing herself for the inevitable boom of thunder ten seconds later.

She waited, totally unprepared for the deafening crack, quickly followed by a huge explosion directly over her head.

Spilling half the water on her nightie, she dropped the glass and bolted for the door, terrified the roof would cave in on her head any second, as every power point sizzled and the heating thermostat on the wall lit up with a loud crackle.

She could barely comprehend what had happened as her survival mechanism kicked in and she fled along the path, her bare feet skidding on the pavers, the rain pelting her skin.

The acrid smell of burning electrics filled her nostrils as she gulped in lungfuls of air, adrenalin pumping as her feet flew up the steps and she fell against Callum's back door, thumping her fists against the glass, screaming as another crash of thunder broke over her.

'Callum!' she shouted, her fists picking up tempo, and suddenly the door opened and she was sobbing against his chest.

'Shh…you're okay. I've got you.'

With a strong arm wrapped around her and a hand stroking her hair she knew she would be, and as her heart-rate calmed she drew great, shuddering breaths, pulling back to swipe at her eyes.

'The storm…lightning hit the cottage…explosion…'

The words tumbled out, almost incoherent, and he nodded.

'I saw it from upstairs. A bolt hit the peak of the roof, exploded a few tiles. I was on my way down when I heard you thumping on the door.'

'You have to do something! Those beautiful furnishings will be ruined. Water might leak inside and—'

'I'll handle it. Will you be okay if I leave you for a moment to go check?'

'Uh-huh.'

She hated how her voice wobbled, and she gave him a gentle shove.

'Go. I'll be right here.'

He hesitated, brushing his thumb across her cheek before grabbing a torch from the nearby mudroom and ducking out into the rain.

Her teeth clattered as she rubbed her bare arms, willing him to come back ASAP, jumping as another crack of thunder boomed over the house.

Belatedly realising how cold and wet she was, she peered out of the back door, trying to see through the sleeting rain, feeling foolish when she realised she couldn't see the cottage behind the towering hedge separating it from the house and pool.

She was jinxed. Destined to lose any home she cared about.

It had happened when she was seven in Adelaide, when her parents had actually stayed in one house for more than a year, and she'd decorated her room with posters and photos and bark paintings she'd made after scouring trees in the nearby hills.

It had happened with the harbourside apartment in Sydney, and now with the cottage—a place she'd stayed less than a fortnight.

'A big fat jinx,' she muttered, her heart leaping as a shadow darted through the rain, then giving an extra twist as she recognised a soggy Callum.

'Is the place okay?'

'Uh-huh. No water damage on the ceiling, but looks like there's a hole in the roof where the tiles exploded.

I'll ring the insurance company and they'll send someone out tonight to tarp it. They can assess the rest of the damage tomorrow.'

He grabbed his mobile off the bench, barely pausing to slick his hair out of his eyes, oblivious to his drenched state.

Her knees started wobbling again, and it had nothing to do with the close call with Mother Nature and everything to do with one very sexy tycoon, his business shirt plastered to his broad chest, his pants clinging to long, lean legs and the droplets clinging to his too-long-to-be-legal eyelashes.

The guy was seriously gorgeous, and if she had to obliterate her fear, focussing on him could do it.

Nothing fazed him. Even now, when most guys would be annoyed their property had been damaged and they'd had to make an impromptu dash into a cyclone-like storm to check it out, he was nothing but commanding and calm and in control.

She liked it. Way too much for comfort.

He glanced across at her, rolled his eyes and made a chattering action with his hand. She could add patience to his list of attributes, especially if the insurance assistant on the other end of the line was being verbose.

'That'll be fine. Just send him out tonight. We'll take care of the rest tomorrow. Right. Thanks.'

He snapped the phone shut, wiped his brow in relief. 'Phew. All that red tape just to get a hole patched in a roof.'

'It's their job.'

She shrugged, suddenly feeling out of place. All she

wanted to do was duck back to the cottage and hide away. Away from gallant, commanding bosses with perceptive eyes.

'What's up?'

'This.' She gestured to the raging storm outside, wincing as another crack of thunder clapped over the house. 'I can't believe it…'

'You can't control the weather. Don't worry, you can move back into the cottage as soon as the roof is fixed.'

The severity of her predicament slammed into her with the force of one of those damn bolts that had caused this mess in the first place.

'You'll stay here, of course.'

She wanted to protest, knew it would be foolish. Of course she'd stay—where else could she go?

It wasn't as if she didn't know Callum. But standing here, watching raindrops glitter on his spiked lashes, seeing the concern in his eyes, she felt as if everything was spinning out of her control and moving way too fast.

'Thanks.'

She managed a wan smile before her teeth gave an almighty clatter and he swore, wrapping an arm around her shoulder and drawing her towards the stairs.

'Come on, you need to get out of that wet nightie.'

'A tried and true line, I'm sure,' she muttered, immediately warmed by his strong arm around her, trying desperately not to lean into him.

'Whatever works.'

She tilted her head to gaze up at him, buoyed by his teasing smile.

Everything would be okay.

She still had a roof over her head, a job and a temporary place to stay. She might have overreacted to the thunderstorm but now, cradled in the comforting crook of Callum's arm, she was infused with a sense of security she'd never experienced before.

He stopped outside a door, released her.

'Guest room. You'll find towels, toiletries and robes in the bathroom. Why don't you take a shower and I'll rustle up some supper?'

'Thanks, but I'm not hungry.'

'Even for designer chocolate?'

'How did you know?'

He smiled and her heart gave another thumpety-thump. 'I spied your stash when I was in the cottage checking for roof damage.'

'Yeah, but that doesn't explain how *you'd* have any.'

His mock-offended expression made her laugh. 'I'll have you know I'm a man of refined tastes.'

'And?'

'My last PA was addicted to the stuff too, and she left it when she eloped with her fella.'

He joined in her chuckles, and despite her uncomfortably clingy nightie, her bedraggled hair and the post-adrenalin exhaustion seeping into her bones, she could have stood there trading banter with him all night.

'You need a shower too.'

She said the first thing that popped into her head, her gaze dipping to the shirt plastered to his chest before wrenching upwards, noting how his dark hair curled when wet, how the rain added a sheen to his bronzed skin.

He was incredible. And she'd be spending the night with him. Spare room or not.

He must have sensed the direction of her thoughts—that or the dribble of saliva escaping her mouth as she drooled over him—for he gave her a gentle shove in the direction of the guest room.

'Go. I'll take a quick shower, then head downstairs to wait for the repair man and rustle up that hot chocolate.'

'Okay, I'll meet you down there.'

He shook his head, reached out to trace a fingertip under her eyes.

'You look beat. Relax up here—go to bed. I'll leave the drink on the bedside table if you're asleep.'

The thought of slipping between clean sheets after a cleansing shower sounded like heaven, yet she hesitated, wondering how she'd ever let him leave the bedroom if he entered it.

As if to remind her she had the energy reserves of a depleted marathon runner she yawned, unable to stifle another.

'Off you go.'

'Bossy,' she muttered, tempering it with a grateful smile.

'Don't you forget it.'

He waited until she'd opened the bedroom door, giving her a funny half-salute before heading down the corridor, leaving her with residual warmth despite her frozen body.

She wasn't supposed to feel anything for this guy. Whatever happened was supposed to be a bit of fun, a transient fling.

Yeah, right—tell that to her stupid, gullible heart, already half in love with him.

CHAPTER NINE

CALLUM knocked softly on the bedroom door before opening it, carefully balancing the supper tray with his other hand. He strained his ears for a response, heard none, and proceeded into the room with caution.

Logically, silence said Starr had drifted off to sleep, just as he'd advised. But nothing in his life had been logical since this blonde dervish had whirled into his life.

He'd been thinking about her, replaying their tension-fraught day, when he'd seen lightning strike the cottage and almost had a heart attack on the spot. He'd never moved so fast, even in his championship hockey days, and all he could think as he ran downstairs was *let her be all right.*

'Callum?'

She sat up in bed, all mussed and ruffled and adorable, her hair tangled, her eyes blinking, her features blurred by sleep, and he'd never seen a woman so desirable.

'Shh…I'll leave your supper here.'

She sat up straighter, rubbed her eyes, and he struggled

to keep his eyes from dipping to the tantalising glimpse of cleavage just visible in the gaping vee of her robe.

She watched him as he neared the bed, and with every step he knew it would damn near impossible to turn around and leave when he'd deposited the tray.

'Smells good.'

'Yeah, it does.'

He wasn't talking about the hot chocolate and toasted cheese sandwich. Rather the seductive scent of rose wafted from the bed towards him, wrapping him in a heady cocoon. Other guests had stayed here, had used the toiletries, but none had smelled as sweetly seductive as Starr.

'Here you go.'

He'd almost completed his mission of leaving the tray and escaping when she rested a hand on his forearm, sending lust licking along his veins.

'Stay.'

His gaze flew to hers, and he was surprised to see a flicker of fear rather than the desire he wished for.

'What's wrong?'

She released him as he sat on the edge of the bed, her fingers plucking at the hand-woven duvet cover.

'It's silly, but I've always been petrified of thunderstorms.'

'You're safe now. And I'm just down the corridor.'

He couldn't stay.

She was asking too much.

What did she think he was? A goddamn saint?

Her teeth worried her bottom lip and he bit back a groan at the swift surge of longing to do the same.

Uh-uh, there was no way in hell he could stay.

Then she raised her eyes to his—wide, luminous blue pools filled with vulnerability.

'Please. I need you to hold me.'

And he was a goner. Just like that.

Mentally uttering a string of creative curses, he opened his arms to her.

'Scoot over.'

She obliged, moving over to give him enough room to slide between the sheets, and as she snuggled into him, a tantalising armful of warm, almost naked woman, he tightened his arms around her, closed his eyes.

It was going to be a long night.

Starr struggled to consciousness, wishing she could slip back into blissful sleep. She'd been suffering insomnia lately, worrying about everything from finding a dance job to finding a permanent place to live, yet last night she'd crashed.

With a relaxed sigh, she snuggled deeper into the covers, savouring the wonderful warmth cushioning her in a cocoon.

Just a few more minutes and she'd get up, start the day with a few stretches as she usually did, before getting ready for work.

Yeah, just a few more minutes... As she wriggled under the covers her cocoon moved and her eyes snapped open, reality crashing with the force of the thunderstorm that had put her here.

She was in bed with Callum.

A very aroused Callum.

A very awake Callum, who was staring at her with a question in his eyes.

A question she should refuse yet to which she wanted to shout a resounding *yes*.

'Morning,' she said, belatedly realising her cocoon consisted of his strong arms holding her tight, his legs entwined with hers, and an unrelenting heat radiating off his body and wrapping her in welcoming warmth.

'Sleep well?'

'Like a baby.'

'I've never really understood that saying.'

He disentangled his limbs from hers, sat up, swinging his legs over the side of the bed and swiping a hand across his eyes while her skin puckered, missing his warmth.

'From what I've heard, babies cry at night and keep their parents up.'

He leaned forward to push off the bed, and she laid a hand on his back, hating the way he stiffened.

'Where are you going?'

'To take a shower. Busy day ahead.'

That was right. They had to ignore the fact he'd spent the night cradling her in his arms, platonic comfort or not, forget they'd done it once before and concentrate on work.

That was exactly what they should do.

Maybe a lightning bolt had hit her as well as the cottage last night, or maybe it was a remnant of a dream, or maybe she just plain yearned to have his arms around her for a few minutes longer. But right that very second she didn't want him to walk away.

Sliding her hand up to his shoulder, she tugged at him until he turned.

'What's your hurry?'

The instant flare of heat in his smouldering gaze sent a shot of anticipation through her. But he instantly damped it, shrugging off her hand.

'This isn't a good time.'

She sat bolt upright, frantically clutching at the sheet before realising she wore the voluminous robe she'd discovered in the guest bedroom closet.

'It never will be.'

He pinned her with the intimidating glare he did so well. 'You're vulnerable right now, not thinking straight.'

Vulnerable? Her? No way. She'd survived worse than one crappy thunderstorm. A lot worse.

'I was shaken last night, that's all. It was nothing.'

She flashed a dazzling smile, tossed her hair, not caring that it must resemble a tangled bird's nest—not the style she went to great lengths to cultivate each morning, with a healthy dollop of hair wax and mousse and the diffuser on her hairdryer.

She wanted to have this out with him. No way would she let him go all righteous on her now.

'You were seriously spooked last night. So don't tell me it was nothing.'

He searched her face for confirmation and she deliberately fixed her smile, ensuring her expression didn't change—something she'd honed through kicking Sergio's sorry butt before leaving him.

Squaring her shoulders, she threw out a challenge she knew he wouldn't refuse.

'You want me.'

There it was: a flash of fire again, and the tiny tic near his jaw indicating she'd scored a direct hit.

'What I want right now is irrelevant. You need to—'

'Don't tell me what I need!'

She jabbed at his chest, hoping to provoke him into touching her right back.

'I *know* what I need. What about you? What do *you* need?'

A battle waged across his face, blinding need warring with saintly intentions, before he reached for her, the heat in his eyes blistering, sending a responding jolt through her body.

'This.'

He pushed her back on the bed, his weight covering her body, the thick length of his erection pushing against her belly as his mouth crushed hers in a desperate kiss that scorched her all the way to her soul.

Her body arched beneath his, surging to meet him, eager to feel him, all of him, deep inside.

But he didn't play fair—uh-uh. While his mouth drove her wild, his tongue meshing with hers, he rolled to one side, giving him room to fully explore her body. His hand tugged at the belt holding her robe together, skimming her skin slick with sweat before gliding lower…lower…

When his fingers delved into her wet folds she groaned, a low, drawn-out moan torn from deep within, as he continued to pleasure her, his thumb expertly circling her clitoris as his fingers slid inside her moist heat.

She was so hot for him, so blindingly in lust, it took less than a minute for him to bring her to climax. The power of it contracted every muscle in her body as she rode crest after crest of sensual pleasure, until she shattered, clutched at him, before collapsing in a wrung-out puddle of loose, languid limbs.

After what seemed like an eternity her eyes fluttered open, caught him staring at her with blatant hunger, before he carefully tugged the gaping edges of the robe together and moved across to the far side of the bed.

She swore. 'Why do you have to be so damn responsible all the time?'

He flinched as if she'd struck him, standing before she could reach out to him.

'Because it's who I am.'

He strode towards the door without looking back, his shoulders rigid, his gait stiff.

'Callum, wait. Don't leave like this. We're not finished…'

He hesitated, shot a quick glance over his shoulder, his expression inscrutable as always.

'Yeah, we are.'

The slamming door echoed the hollow in her heart.

'Is the cottage safe?'

'Safe as houses.'

The electrician grinned at his corny pun, but Callum wasn't amused. He wanted the cottage back to normal ASAP, so his unexpected house guest could resume residential status there.

He'd been like a madman all morning, hassling the insurance company, demanding the roof be fixed and the wiring checked. They'd complied, and now he could deliver the good news to Starr.

He needed her out of his house, out of proximity, out of touching distance…before he lost his mind.

He'd almost blown it this morning.

Waking up with her in his arms, soft and warm and pliant, he'd experienced such an overwhelming surge of longing it had left him breathless.

But the longing hadn't been purely physical, and that was what scared him the most, what had sent him running after he'd pleasured her, what drove him to put as much emotional distance between them as possible.

He didn't do emotions—not any more.

'I'll put my report in to the insurance company, but you'll be right, mate. Nothing to fix. You were lucky.'

Yeah, real lucky—discounting the fact that in one long night his exuberant, feisty PA had shown him a new side to her, a glimpse of vulnerability, and wangled her way into his hardened heart.

'Thanks.'

'No worries.'

The electrician saluted before hoisting his toolbox and setting off down the path leading to the main driveway, leaving him staring at the cottage and pondering the real reason behind Starr's freak-out.

Lightning striking the roof would have made a god-awful noise, but her reaction had been surprising—especially considering her resilience.

She'd packed up and headed to a new city, taking a less-than-ideal job, and she was making the most of it. Confident, bold and fearless, she was the least likely woman to be affected by a simple thunderstorm.

Yet she hadn't wanted him to leave her alone last night, and he'd seen the genuine fear in her eyes.

Thank goodness his shredded self-control had kicked in. And yet this morning, after having her wriggling against him half the night and torturing his howling libido in the process, he'd cracked.

Kissing her, touching her, making her climax, had shaken him to his core.

He'd had her naked and willing in his arms, matching him every step of the way, but when he'd seen her lying against the sheets, glowing and sated and defenceless, something had reached deep down, grabbed hold of his heart and twisted hard.

He didn't want to feel anything for her—wanted to make sure if they had sex again it would be how he usually liked it: hot, fierce, unemotional.

But having her in his house, dependent on him for shelter as well as her job, was too much.

After what had happened this morning he wasn't a complete fool.

Despite all his protestations, all the logical reasons

why they shouldn't get involved, they'd have sex again. It was just a matter of when.

Though he'd make damn sure the next time it would be a wild, fun ride without a hint of emotion in sight.

CHAPTER TEN

'YOU'VE been holding out on me, bro.'

Callum sighed, pinched the bridge of his nose, glad to get another call from Rhys but wishing his timing was better.

He'd had a rotten morning, unable to concentrate on anything other than the beautiful woman sitting opposite, with battle-squared shoulders and determination in her eyes.

She hadn't mentioned what had happened first thing this morning. She didn't have to.

It was written all over her face.

She was going to make his life miserable until he did what he should have done after that first kiss by the pool.

Gave in.

'What are you talking about?'

'Who's the hot babe who answered the phone? She doesn't seem like your usual type.'

Grateful Starr had taken a lunch break out of the office, he sat back.

'Starr's my PA.'

'Is that all?'

'Two words for you. Back off.'

Rhys did what he'd always done when faced with an order. He laughed.

'Come on, Cal, if you're this wound up you must fancy her. Why don't you go for it?'

Therein lay the problem.

He'd already 'gone for it', as his younger brother so delicately put it, and rather than easing his need for her she was now all he could think about every waking moment. And most sleepless ones too.

Starr was fast becoming more than the type of woman to 'go for it' with, and he didn't like the feelings she stirred up. He didn't want to feel any emotions where she was concerned—wanted it to be a bit of fun for however long she stayed here.

'Oh-oh.'

'What?'

'You really like this one.'

'What if I do?'

'What happened to your "never get involved" motto? I've never heard you mention a woman, let alone allow me to rib you like this. What gives?'

'I'm not involved.'

His hollow rebuttal only served to reinforce how much he already was.

'Not buying it, bro.'

Rhys was the only sibling he had now—exactly why he put up with his jesting when he wouldn't from anyone else.

'Did you want anything in particular, or were you just ringing to make my life miserable?'

Rhys chuckled. 'I just wanted to make sure you were cool.'

He knew exactly what Rhys was talking about.

The anniversary of Archie's death always brought them closer. He might not hear from Rhys for months on end, but when February twenty-third rocked around every year he would start calling more frequently.

It hurt as much as it felt good—knowing he had a brother who cared, knowing he'd robbed Rhys of a sibling.

When Archie had been alive he'd been a dynamo, a giant of a man both physically and in the business world. When Archie Cartwright had entered a room, people had sat up and taken notice. He'd dwarfed everyone and everything around him, yet never made his younger brothers feel second-best.

Archie had looked out for him, looked out for them both, had understood why he'd been hell-bent on drinking and carousing his way through his teens.

Yet he'd never judged, never preached, just always been there for him.

And it had ultimately got him killed.

It was why Callum strove to be the best every day since his senseless death, to be the type of guy Archie would want him to be.

Sometimes he envied Rhys, who'd coped with his grief by running away. They'd both been the adventurous ones, and while he'd taken on Archie's business re-

sponsibilities Rhys had travelled continents, staying the
hell away from home.

Thank God his parents were doing the same.

'Yeah, I'm cool. You?'

'No worries here.'

He clamped down on the urge to push. Rhys needed
looking out for, needed guidance, needed a steadying in-
fluence. He owed him that much after robbing the kid
of his eldest brother.

'Good. If you need anything don't hesitate to holler.'

He wanted to wipe the memory of Rhys's stunned,
wounded puppy expression, which had lingered for the
first year after Archie died, and would do anything and
everything in his power to make his brother happy.

But Rhys was an independent soul—something he
understood, something he missed—and he hated how a
small part of him still wished he could leave all this
behind and return to the life he'd once had.

'No worries. Later, bro. And say bye to that sexy PA.'

He clenched the phone as the dial tone hummed in
his ears.

Sexy PA?

Rhys didn't know the half of it.

Callum glanced up from the spreadsheets scattered
across his desk, linked fingers stretched overhead.

Time to quit.

And set his plan in motion.

'We're finished for the day.'

Starr held up a finger, jotted down something on a

sticky-note, before pushing back from her desk and twirling her seat around—twice, for good measure—her long legs extended, drawing attention to her shapely calves, making him swallow.

'Good. All these figures are sending me cross-eyed.'

She wasn't the only one. Though it was one figure in particular in this office that was sending him cross-eyed, and he was looking straight at it.

'Plenty more where that came from. I've left you a ton of work while I'm away next week.'

She grimaced. 'You're pushing it.'

No, but he was about to.

'You're going to be virtually stuck in here for the next seven days, which is exactly why we should go out tonight.'

'Go out?'

To give her credit she recovered quickly, her dazed expression replaced by a genuinely happy smile.

'We're going out tonight.' He folded his arms, confident in his plan. 'On a date, in case you were wondering.'

'A date?'

'That's right, a date. You know—that thing two people do when they fancy each other. And when one of them screws up badly.'

He swiped a hand across his face, wishing he could wipe away the memory of walking out on her that morning as easily.

'I'm sorry for botching this morning.'

'Apology accepted.'

She tapped her lips, pretended to think. 'You know, I guess we never got around to the dating part.'

Exactly why he was doing this.

It didn't sit well with him, the fact he hadn't treated her like a lady, and hot on the heels of his post-storm freak-out he wanted to do this right.

'No, we didn't. That first night—well…there was no dating involved. And we haven't been in sync since.'

She leaned forward, and he fought a tremendous battle to stay focussed on her face and not sneak a peek at the hint of cleavage on tantalising display.

'I know the perfect way for us to get in *sync*.'

So did he, and the thought of sweeping everything off his desk and going for it had the blood pounding in his ears.

Crooking her finger at him, she dropped her voice to just above a whisper.

'Dancing. You and me. After our dinner date.'

The memory of her swaying in time to the music in the ballroom flashed across his mind—the way she'd raised her arms overhead, moved her hips…

Shifting in his chair, he pointed to his Italian handmade shoes.

'What if I have two left feet?'

'We'll improvise.'

Her husky innuendo hung in the air, tempting, teasing, and he struggled not to blurt *screw the date* and take her right here, right now.

Glancing at his watch, he said, 'How long will it take you to get ready?'

'Give me five minutes to change and I'm all yours.'

'I'll hold you to that,' he murmured, anticipation mounting as she sauntered from the room with an extra swivel to her hips.

Callum was a dream date.

Charming, attentive, witty. Throw in long meaningful looks from those gorgeous brown eyes, the occasional finger-brushing across the table, the constant buzz of sexual tension, and she knew she was in *waaaay* over her head with this one.

They'd made it through dinner. Dancing was her forte, and should have given her the upper hand. With a guy like Callum she should have known better.

'Interesting place.'

His arm stayed glued to her waist as they entered the dimly lit jazz club, the blues beat instantly giving her itchy feet.

'How did you find it?'

'The E-guide online. Said this was the best jazz bar in town.'

'So you're a fan?'

'Huge.'

'Me too.'

She didn't know why this common bond thrilled her, was aware she shouldn't care so much, but she did, and the faster she got him out of here and into her bed—if only to prove their connection was purely physical—the easier her conscience could rest.

For, no matter how many times she silently chastised herself that the buzz between them now was merely a leftover remnant of that memorable night in Sydney, she knew better.

'Let's dance.'

Just one quick spin around the floor. She couldn't stand much more of the tension, nor the constant nagging inner voice that continually whispered *you're in too deep*.

He stopped dead, his serious expression belied by the naughty gleam in his eyes.

'I lied to you.'

'About?'

He bumped her gently with his hip, pointed to his shoes. 'I don't have two left feet.'

'Proof of the pudding and all that.'

'I was junior state ballroom dancing champion for two years straight in high school.'

'You can *dance?*'

His self-effacing smile merely added to his charm. 'Don't sound so surprised. Do I look like a clumsy oaf to you?'

What he looked like was the ultimate dreamboat—every girl's fantasy come to life.

'Now you're just fishing for compliments.'

Tossing her hair, she took his outstretched hand. Could he be any more perfect? Next he'd be saying he adored sushi and funky jewellery and long, decadent baths.

With a toe-curling smile, he said, 'Is it working?'

'I have a feeling you know exactly how good you are.'

'Hey, a guy can never have too much reassurance.'

'Come on, Mr Ballroom Champ, let's see what you're made of.'

Tugging on her hand until she was plastered against his chest, he said, 'I'm up for the challenge if you are.'

'I'm up for anything.'

She pinned him with a sultry stare, leaving him in little doubt as to what she meant.

Brushing the barest of kisses against her lips, he murmured, 'Then let's make this dance quick and get out of here.'

Finally, *finally,* they were on the same page. Trouble was she knew what the next chapter held, but what about the one after that? And would this page-turner have a happy ending?

As the sexy, soulful music filtered through the club Callum held her tight, his feet never faulting as he guided her through a perfect rumba.

She should have been in her element, oblivious to everything but the music taking her to the special place it always did, but with Callum's arms around her, his body deliciously close, all she could focus on was him. Only him.

As the music changed, he released her, tipped up her chin.

'Care to rate my performance?'

'On a scale of one to ten?'

'Sure.'

Trailing a fingertip down his cheek, she said, 'Nine point five.'

'What did I lose the half-point for?'

'Doing the dance upright.'

His eyes widened, darkened at the innuendo, and before she could lose the advantage, along with her bravado, she grabbed his hand and made a break for the door.

CHAPTER ELEVEN

'I'D FORGOTTEN how nice this place is.'

'Nice?' Starr glanced up at him, incredulous. 'It's gorgeous!'

Callum chuckled, hugged her closer as they stepped into the lounge room. 'Guess I never come down here.'

'Never?'

'No reason to—unless the place gets hit by stray bolts of lightning.'

She shuddered, and he mentally kicked himself for bringing it up.

'Don't remind me. Coffee?'

'Sure. Need a hand?'

Her mischievous grin set his pulse pounding in an instant. 'Maybe later.'

Excited by her boldness, he watched her dance around the kitchen, circling here, promenading there, every movement lithe and elegant and bewitching as she performed the otherwise mundane task of putting the kettle on to boil, filling cups.

He could admire her fluid grace all night, but now he

was here he couldn't fathom the strange restlessness gripping him.

He had to be up early tomorrow, catching a plane interstate, and the thought of having sex with Starr and then running out of here on a tight timeline didn't sit well with him.

She deserved to be held, caressed, cherished all night long, but he couldn't afford the time, couldn't allow business to slip. The upcoming deal was too important to botch, no matter how tempting the distraction.

'Does anyone else ever stay here?'

He took the coffee mug from her hands. 'Thanks. You're the first.'

Her mouth curved into a beguiling smile. 'Lucky me.'

With his gaze focussed on her mouth, a mouth made for sin, he knew he was the lucky one. And about to get a whole lot luckier.

She cupped her mug, took a sip, her enquiring gaze never leaving his.

'So what's this big deal you have going down next week?'

'A possible merger between another finance company and Cartwrights.'

'Sounds big.'

'Huge.'

Her eyes sparkled with mischief. 'Must be some serious work, considering you're booked at a Whitsunday island for a week.'

He shrugged. For all he cared he could be stuck in Timbuktu when he was conducting business.

'These guys like to be schmoozed.'

'Half their luck.'

'Are we going to talk work all night?'

She laid down her coffee mug, unfurled her long legs from the chair opposite to come and sit beside him. Her subtle floral fragrance enveloped him, bewitched him.

'I'm naturally nosy.' She nudged his arm playfully, trying to lighten the mood. 'One of my few faults.'

Grateful for the diversion, he drained his coffee before placing the mug on the coffee table.

'Any others?'

'Hmm…let me see.'

She tapped her bottom lip—a temptingly full bottom lip he had every intention of savouring shortly.

'I have a weakness for sushi, eclectic jewellery, dance shoes and tall, good-looking, commanding men.' She ticked the list off on her fingers, beaming at him. 'Not necessarily in that order.'

'Men, huh?'

Her eyes lost their teasing sparkle, darkened to a beguiling sapphire.

'Well, maybe just one man in particular.'

Reaching out, he trailed a finger along her cheek, her jaw, her collarbone, enjoying the first flicker of awareness in her smouldering gaze, the sharp intake of breath that signalled she was as ready for this as he was.

'I'm hoping you're looking straight at him.'

'Uh-huh,' she said, a second before she leaped at him, captured his face and kissed him silly.

He loved her spontaneity, her vibrancy, and in that moment it felt great to relinquish control.

As she straddled him, deepened the kiss, teasing his tongue to match hers, making him harder with every little moan escaping her mouth, he realised a lot could be said for losing control. A hell of a lot.

Driven by weeks of pent-up frustration, he almost ripped the tight red dress off her body, raining frantic kisses all over her body, her breasts, his mouth wild, his hands everywhere, caressing her smooth skin, getting reacquainted.

'You feel incredible.'

He moaned as she cupped his erection through his trousers, her fingernails scraping the zip, deliberately provocative.

'So do you.'

A loud metal rip, followed by her heat-seeking hand zeroing in on him, pushed him closer to the edge, and he swept her into his arms, deposited her on the four-poster bed and braced himself over her.

'Let me look at you.'

Her hands skimmed his chest, moulding, exploring, and he gritted his teeth as she headed lower again.

'Later. I want you. Now.'

'I like this bossy side of you,' he said, peeling her panties off, all the breath whooshing out of him at the sight of her lying naked in front of him.

'Good. You'll like this even more.'

With a quick grab and roll she reversed positions, her

proud grin turning wicked as her heated gaze started at his chest and worked its way down.

'You won't need these.'

She whipped off his trousers, quickly followed by his briefs, and he groaned as she sheathed him, the pressure building, his self-control in tatters.

'Still liking the bossy thing?'

'Loving it,' he managed to say as her hot entrance hovered over him before sliding down, inch by torturous inch, until she enclosed him in liquid velvet.

'Me too.'

They didn't speak after that, didn't need to, as he gripped her hips, arched upwards, driving into her while she rode him with her head thrown back, her breasts jiggling and her hands gripping his forearms. He memorised the moment, taking a mental erotic snapshot of this unforgettable woman.

Her enthusiasm was a major turn-on and he picked up the pace, felt her tightening around him the moment before she shattered, screaming his name, followed a second later by his own mind-blowing climax.

She was right. It paid to let someone else be in charge every now and then.

'I have to go.'

She stretched, languid and sated and incredibly beautiful.

'So soon?'

He nodded, hating how wrong this felt—him bolting like a fugitive into the night.

'Early flight, and loads to do before then, considering I was distracted last night.'

'You complaining?'

She rolled onto her side, propped on one elbow, the sheet delicately draped over her breasts, and he swallowed, knowing if he didn't make his escape now he'd never leave.

'No complaints here.'

Their gazes met, locked, two people in perfect sync, and that scared him more than the urge to stay.

'I'll be back in a week.'

'After I've tackled that suitably long list of tasks you've left for me.'

'I'm a busy man. Would you expect anything less?'

'No.'

He hesitated, confounded by the strange, driving urge to stay.

He'd never had this compulsion before, had slept with women who knew the score, who were only too happy for him to leave and head home to his own bed.

But here, now, watching Starr propped on one elbow, her tousled hair spilling in tempting waves across her shoulders, the sheet draped provocatively over her breasts, rooted his feet to the spot.

'What's up?'

He frowned, unable to articulate what he was feeling, annoyed he was feeling it in the first place.

'Don't even think about going all weird on me after last night, because—'

'Come with me.'

She sat up, not caring when the sheet slipped, making a belated grab for it when his gaze strayed south.

'What?'

Damn, he'd blurted his innermost thoughts and now it was too late to take it back.

He had to concentrate this next week, ensure this deal happened, and having his sexy PA along would do nothing but distract.

'Why don't you come with me? There'll be loads of work, but you'll have time to unwind too.'

A flicker of guilt stabbed him. Work wasn't the only reason he wanted her along.

Now he'd had another taste of this delectable woman he wanted her by his side, all night long, for as many nights as she had left here.

'You're asking me to go away with you?'

'On a business trip.'

Her lips curved into a smug smile at his clarification, recognising it for the dubious excuse it was.

'Well then, when you put it like that, I guess I can't refuse my boss.'

With the elegance of a queen draped in regal robes, she wound the sheet around her lissom body and stood, gliding towards him like a Grecian goddess.

'Before we get caught up in *business,* last night was just as special as Sydney.' Her hungry gaze focussed on his mouth before dragging upwards to his eyes. 'I just wanted you to know that.'

'Come here.'

He hauled her into his arms, his fingers tangling in

her hair as he angled her head, crushing his mouth to hers, his driving need for her needing little to reignite.

She clung to him, matching his hunger, matching him in every way, and, terrified by the thought, he tore his mouth from hers, dragging in air to clear his head.

Laughing, she trailed a fingertip down his chest. 'This is going to be one hell of a week.'

His sentiment exactly.

CHAPTER TWELVE

STARR sauntered into the separate office of their beach-
side bungalow, determined to distract her workaholic
boss. They'd already put in a solid eight hours today—
time for a little R and R.

She hadn't bought his business trip spiel. Sure, he
might like having his PA along to assist with work stuff
for the week on Hayman Island, but the way they'd
been burning up the sheets she knew the real reason he'd
invited her along.

He couldn't get enough of her, and the feeling was
mutual.

He hadn't heard her. His head bent, he had a pen in
his right hand, rapidly scrawling notes. The sight of
him was enough to set her heart flip-flopping and send
her belly into free-fall.

The guy was seriously hot, from the top of his
slicked-back dark hair to the soles of his designer shoes.

She'd never gone for guys in suits, preferring the
more casual look of the artsy-fartsy dance crowd. Guys
in faded denim and tight T-shirts, guys with layered

jackets and scarves, guys with hair just a tad too long to be conventional.

Callum was none of those things, was always immaculately dressed in crisp shirts and conservative ties and posh suits, his hair neat in the short back-and-sides, without a scarf in sight. Yet she wanted him more than any of those other guys, wanted him more than Sergio, and she'd lived with him for a few years.

'Hey, it's knock-off time.'

He glanced up from a stack of paperwork and her heart squirmed all over again.

'How late is it?'

She sashayed across the room, thankful she'd changed into her favourite floral bikini and sheer cover-all, delighting in his dazed expression. If her working it in this bikini didn't take his mind off business, nothing would.

'Late enough for you to shut down that computer and come take a dip.'

'Swimming, huh?'

He stood, stretched, sinfully gorgeous as he rounded the desk, his hungry expression wrenching an answering response deep down.

'I'd rather stay in.'

Before she could respond he kissed her, a savage, wild, no-holds-barred kiss that shook her all the way down to her soul.

This thing between them was more than physical, way more, and as she clung to him, matched him, fired him by clambering all over him, she knew that falling for him had been a foregone conclusion right from the very beginning.

He backed her up against the desk, the evidence of why he wanted to stay in pressing into her pelvis.

'So we're done for the day?'

'We're only just getting started,' he murmured against her neck, his hot, moist kisses sending shivers of need through her.

'Now you're talking.'

She wanted this, wanted him desperate and panting for her, unable to get enough.

But she couldn't dismiss her conscience all together.

'You make that conference call to London yet?'

'Forget about the conference call.'

She couldn't agree more.

'Good attitude.'

With a wide sweep of her arm she sent the documents covering the desk crashing to the floor, enjoying the clatter of pens against the polished wood.

'Wow, I've always wanted to do that.'

'And I've always wanted to do this.'

She'd expected him to be annoyed to have his precious work strewn across the floor. Instead he picked her up, placed her butt on the desk and ripped open her cover-all.

'Hey! That's the only cover-all I own.'

'Tough. Besides, you won't need it. I much prefer you strutting around in a bikini anyway.'

'I like the way you think.'

'And I love the way you feel.'

His fingertips skated across her skin, dipping

between her breasts, teasing her nipples through the bikini bra.

'And taste.'

He dipped his head, his mouth replacing his hands, nipping the swell of her breasts, tender little bites that tore a low moan from her throat.

'And sound.'

His mouth covered hers in a blistering kiss that reached down to her soul and beyond, and she gave herself over to the mind-blowing pleasure of making love with a master hell-bent on her pleasure.

Thanks to Callum, she'd discovered more about her body, about sensual pleasure, than she'd ever dreamed possible.

A small part of her had thought the lacklustre sex with Sergio had been her fault, but Callum had blasted that misconception with every expert touch of his hands, his tongue.

She couldn't get enough—couldn't get enough of him.

When he'd untied her top, he feasted on her breasts for an inordinate amount of time until she writhed and groaned beneath him, begging for more.

When he peeled off her bikini bottoms she lay splayed on the desk, not caring how wanton she looked, desperate for him—all of him.

And when he finally plunged into her, again and again and again, each time harder and deeper than the last, she came apart within moments.

'That was unbelievable.'

He collapsed against her, held her close, her legs

wrapped tightly around his waist, the welcome hardness of him still buried within her, and for a long, exquisite moment in time she found the security she'd always craved.

Callum perused the same spreadsheet for the tenth time in the last few minutes, his mind wandering from the figures at hand to the figure he'd like in his hands.

He'd never been this distracted, had never allowed anything or anyone to distract from his goals. And his goals were clear: make Cartwright Corporation the number one financial institute in the country, be a suitable stand-in for Archie, stay in control always.

Right now his goals were teetering.

Bringing Starr to Hayman Island had been a bad move, and if he continued dwelling on her business would suffer.

He wanted her, every second of every day.

Madness.

He was obsessed with her, would find his mind drifting as she took notes, would find erotic memories filtering across his mind while discussing an agenda.

His fabled control was shot, along with any chance he had of fooling himself this was nothing but a fling.

Working together, playing together this last week, had him craving her more than ever.

Which begged the question: what would happen when they returned to Melbourne, she inevitably found a job in dance, and left?

What then?

He didn't do relationships, couldn't promise a woman anything beyond physical pleasure. Getting emotionally involved wasn't an option.

So how the hell had he landed in this predicament?

He snapped to attention the second Starr entered the conference room, schooling his expression into one of polite welcome, masking the raging desperation to touch her every time he laid eyes on her.

'The Japanese investors should be here shortly.'

'Paperwork ready?'

She laughed, strutted across the room in that flamboyant style he loved, her feathery layered skirt swishing about her shapely calves, her nimble, supple dancer's body an enticing part of her allure.

'Of course. Have you ever found me anything but efficient?'

'Good point.'

'Anything else you'd like me to do? Last-minute jobs?'

He could think of a few, but none that wouldn't earn him a hard slap.

'Relax, you've earned it.'

She propped herself on the end of his desk, kinked her hip out, fixed him with a provocative stare that could have tempted a monk.

'I've been pretty indispensable, huh?'

'No one's indispensable.'

He'd learned that the hard way too, being thrust into the CEO position at Cartwright Corporation way too early, replacing the legendary Archie Cartwright whom everyone had thought irreplaceable.

'Come on, can't you humour a girl?'

Matching her flirtatious wink, he stood, strode around the desk until they were toe to toe.

'I can think of other things I'd rather be doing with this girl.'

She held up her hands, as if that would stop him, her laugh husky.

'Think of your reputation, Mr Cartwright. This is a place of business.'

Ducking his head for a snatched kiss, he murmured, 'It's also a very hot tropical island, and I want you wearing less clothes by the time I get back to the bungalow.'

Batting her eyelashes, she said, 'Is that an order?'

'You bet.'

'In that case I'd better do as I'm told.'

She slid off the desk, slipped her arms around him. 'Wouldn't want to get the boss offside.'

She was joking, teasing him as she usually did, but the closer they got, the more he hated being her boss. They had such an unconventional relationship—had moved from a one-night stand to work colleagues to lovers.

It all seemed skewed, somehow, and for someone who liked everything clear-cut he didn't like feeling this bamboozled.

'What's wrong?'

She released him, stepped back, confusion creasing her brow.

'I'm just tense about this upcoming meeting.'

Her eyes narrowed, her mouth pursed in a cute scoff.

'There's more to it.'

Damn right there was more. More confusion, more delusion, more headaches the longer he contemplated where they went from here.

Could they sustain a serious relationship once they returned to Melbourne?

It would be his first, the first time he'd let a woman get close, and if that wasn't hard enough she wasn't his type.

She was too feisty, too fiery, too vibrant—the type of woman to make his life hell. If he ever settled down it should be with someone malleable, agreeable, biddable. Someone who wouldn't oppose him, confound him, confuse him.

He liked his life orderly.

He liked his life calm and structured and controlled.

But what if he liked Starr more?

The thought jarred, jolted, unnerved him. And he did the only thing possible when confronted by feelings he'd rather not have, let alone acknowledge.

He reverted to what he knew best: business.

'I have to get back to work.'

She snorted, her familiar sass evident in the flash of fire in her blue eyes, the toss of her hair.

'Of course you do.'

He deliberately glanced at his watch. 'I'll see you back at the bungalow later.'

Her eyes narrowed, sparked, shot him down.

She was magnificent.

'Only if you're lucky.'

'What's that supposed to mean?'

She pinned him with an exasperated glare.

'Just finish your work. We'll catch up later.'

He should let her go, let her walk out of here just as he wanted, but the faintest flicker of hurt in her eyes had him snagging her hand, splaying it against his chest.

'Sorry for being a bore.'

Her fingers flexed against his chest, gripping his shirt as if she didn't want to let go, tightening the emotional noose around his neck further.

'I promise I'll make it up to you later. Okay?'

'You better.'

Her emphatic nod sent a tumble of golden waves cascading around her face and he pushed them back, unable to resist, unable to do anything but wind his fingers through the messy silken locks, wishing he was doing this in the bungalow's king-size bed with the two of them naked.

Tugging gently, he brought her head towards him, leaned forward and rested his forehead against hers, hoping even half of what he was thinking and feeling would magically get across to her.

When he finally straightened, what seemed like an eternity later, the naked yearning on her face hit him right where he feared it most.

His heart.

'You're killing me, you know that?'

She bit her bottom lip—a vulnerable gesture at odds with her usual confidence.

'Why? Because I won't back away, no matter how hard you push?'

Sorry hovered on his lips, begged to be said, but he bit it back, swallowed it. This wasn't the time or the place to get into a discussion about why he did half the things he did.

The insidious niggling of that treacherous organ in his chest told him he'd need to come clean soon, would need to give her some semblance of the truth before she walked, taking more of him with her than he'd ever thought possible.

Brushing a kiss across her lips, he murmured, 'Later.'

'I'll hold you to that.'

She patted his cheek, the gesture more affectionate, more intimate somehow, than anything they'd done to date, and his heart lurched.

Not only had he let his reservations slide this week, they'd crashed and burned as they'd slipped into an easy relationship—one where they worked together during the day and unwound together at night over sensational seafood caught fresh from the Barrier Reef, followed by dessert: hours of sensational sex.

She knew he liked the right side of the bed.

She knew he needed at least three short black coffees to be coherent in the mornings.

She knew he liked to pleasure her first before his climax.

It was too much too soon, and for him to let his guard down around any woman, let alone this one, spoke volumes.

'I'll see you later.'

She dropped a quick peck on his lips, slipped out of his

arms, and while his attention should be fixed on the investors' meeting ahead, he found it firmly fixed on one incredibly sexy woman as she strolled out through the door.

The meeting with the Japanese investors went better than expected, but rather than getting away early, as he'd hoped, he'd be stuck here for the next few hours.

It wouldn't normally bother him, but he felt like a heel for treating Starr so dismissively earlier and he wanted to make it up to her.

Grabbing his mobile, he hit the 'recall' button, waited for it to ring, drumming his fingers against the table.

He had a stack of preparation to do before tomorrow's meeting, a conference call to schedule and a load of contracts to peruse, but all of that could wait.

Right now he had a more pressing engagement, and he wouldn't take no for an answer.

'Why, hello there.'

His libido jerked to attention at the sound of Starr's sultry tone, reminiscent of some screen siren he once lusted over.

'How did you know it was me?'

'Amazing thing, caller ID.'

Her soft chuckles raised the hairs on his neck and he rubbed it.

'Besides, you never know when I might need a handsome CEO.'

'Just handsome?'

'Technicalities.'

He loved this: her spontaneity, her flirting, her ability

to turn the mundane into something bright and sparkling and funny.

'What are your plans for tonight?'

'That depends.'

'On?'

'If you're asking me to do some catch-up filing, I'm
washing my hair.'

Her pause promised the world.

'Though if you're asking me if I'm busy because
you have some nefarious plans you'd like a willing and
able partner for, then I'm free.'

'Good. In that case, I'm taking you out.'

'How can a girl refuse an offer like that?'

Her soft tone held a hint of mystery and magic and
he could hardly wait.

'You can't. I'm going to be stuck here longer than
expected, so I'll swing by the bungalow at seven.'

'Where are we going?'

He glanced at the brochure one of the resort staff
had given him.

'You'll find out.'

Her exasperated sigh made him smile. She didn't
take kindly to orders, and his being tight-lipped would
be killing her.

'What should I wear?'

With anticipation pumping through his veins at the
thought of seeing her later, he lowered his tone.

'That's easy. Something sexy.'

He only just caught her sharp exhalation as he

snapped the phone shut, thrust it in his pocket and busied himself with finishing off the day's work.

Tonight he'd make sure Starr was left in little doubt this trip wasn't all business.

aged the phone, hung this time in his pocket and pasted a nonchalant expression on the way s she...

Trouble in paradise sure signal whatever dump her up wasn't all business.

CHAPTER THIRTEEN

STARR PACED THE bungalow veranda, stopped to stare out at the gorgeous ocean view, the pristine white sand, the lush greenery, jiggling from one foot to the other.

She hated waiting—hated feeling like this more. Not that she could articulate what *this* was, other than a confounding mix of blinding excitement, raging lust and soul-deep yearning.

Callum confused the heck out of her: flirting one second, pushing her away the next. He'd lightened up so much this past week, almost been a different man, yet the way he'd looked at her this afternoon... intense, annoyed, as if he was waging some huge inner battle.

Confused? She was completely bamboozled. But there was little doubt in her mind now that what they had had gone beyond the physical. Way beyond.

Where did that leave her?

She'd already lost one job and a home, courtesy of letting her heart rule her head, so what would happen if she got too involved here?

She loved living in the cottage, was thankful she finally had some money as a safety net.

And, while they'd connected on so many levels here on the island, she couldn't shake the fear that once they returned to Melbourne Callum would revert to his stoic, solid best, content to focus on business, effectively shutting her out.

The signs were there. He'd pushed her away this afternoon when she'd got too close and, while he'd apologised, it didn't change the fact she was scared. Heck, she was downright terrified he'd walk away from her without a backward glance at the end of all this.

Bringing her back full circle to her original worry: would she be back to where she'd started—homeless, jobless, penniless—when this fantasy they were living on the island crashed with the finesse of a high-kicking hora gone wrong?

The rumbling engine of one of the resort's carts caught her attention, and she peered out into the dusk, her heart leaping when Callum's cart slid to a stop in front of the bungalow.

He left the engine idling as he stepped from the cart and around it to open her door. She let him, impressed by his chivalry. She might be a modern woman, but having an old-fashioned guy spoil her went a long way.

'Ready for a night you'll never forget?'

'Bet you say that to all the girls.'

'Only ones in dresses short enough to pass as crop-tops.'

'You like?'

She didn't tug the hem of her sequined primrose mini-dress down, enjoying his lingering stare on her thighs too much.

'Oh, I like. Very much.'

He didn't touch her—didn't need to. Her skin was tingling under the heat from his stare until she squirmed in her seat.

'So where are you taking me?'

'It's a surprise.'

'Good. You know how much I love them.'

'Yeah, I know.'

His low voice rippled over her and she swallowed, unable to ignore the growing feeling she was in over her head.

She wanted to have fun tonight, wanted to enjoy their last few nights, wanted to set the foundation for a possible future back in Melbourne, to see if they had anything substantial between them beyond a spark.

Spark? More like a raging bonfire, and if he didn't put the cart into gear shortly they'd be right back to where they started: getting naked without talking first.

Slapping the dash with a healthy dose of fake bravado, she said, 'Let's hit the road. Surprise time.'

His intense gaze lingered a second longer before he smiled, focussed on steering the cart.

'Starr?'

'Hmm?'

'I'm really looking forward to tonight.'

Her heart rolled over, lay down and yelled *pick me!* at the sincerity in his tone, and she reached across, squeezed his hand on the steering wheel, unable to resist touching him a second longer.

'Me too.'

Callum had it all planned out.

Take Starr to a fancy dinner at the water's edge, followed by a romantic stroll along the beach, finish with dancing into the wee small hours.

A date she'd enjoy, a date to impress, a date to show how much he cared.

So much for planning.

'You sure I can't carry you to the cart?'

Shooting him an 'are you for real?' glance, she shook her head.

'That'd be taking your knight in shining armour routine too far.'

Knight? He couldn't feel further from one if he tried.

The five-star meal at the water's edge had turned soggy when they'd borne the brunt of a freak tropical downpour, then they'd fielded some unwelcome guests in the form of ravenous mosquitoes, and their romantic beach stroll had taken a serious nosedive when the heel on one of her shoes had caught in the sand and snapped.

So here they were, limping up the beach: she was limping literally, his pride figuratively. He'd never botched an evening out with a lady so badly.

'It's no big deal, you know.'

Great—she must have picked up on his surly mood.

'I wanted tonight to be—'

'Special.' She stopped, slipped her hand into his and squeezed. 'It has been.'

'How can you say that? The food got drenched, the mozzies were annoying, and—'

'Look around.'

She gestured towards the ocean with her free hand, the broken shoe dangling forlornly from her fingertip a stark reminder of his broken dreams for tonight.

'It's a beautiful evening, we're on a fabulous island, and we're together. What more could you ask for?'

Buoyed by her constant optimism, he followed her line of vision, seeing the twinkling resort lights against a midnight sky, the endless ocean, the hulking shape of a mountain range.

He never took time out to admire his surroundings, considered Melbourne the business capital of Australia rather than the capital of the Garden State, as Victoria was known. As for leisurely strolls—try never.

Inhaling the pungent scents of fresh seafood and tapas and decadent desserts assailing him from a resort restaurant nearby, he wondered what it was about this woman that made him see and smell and feel everything differently.

At that moment the first strains of a soulful sax filtered towards them and he closed his eyes, hanging onto her hand for dear life, hanging onto the last of his resistance more.

He'd fought this.

Fought it with every rebellious cell in his tightly wound, tightly controlled body.

But he was a realist, if nothing else, and spending time with Starr tonight, after missing her in every second spent away from her when they weren't working or playing together the last few days, cemented what he already knew.

He was in love with her.

And there wasn't one damn thing he could do about it.

'Callum?'

His eyes snapped open, focussed on her face. Her beauty slugged him anew. In the soft moonlight reflected off the water's edge her eyes sparkled like blue diamonds, her lips curved into a half-coy, half-sexy smile, her hair was wild and tousled.

He wanted her so badly he ached, but he needed to save what was left of this disastrous first date, needed to prove he was as successful at this as everything else.

'Dance with me?'

Her eyebrows shot up, her delighted surprise vindicating his decision to let down his famed guard and do something totally out of character.

'Here?'

He nodded, his gaze never leaving hers, hoping she could read half of what he was feeling, all of what he couldn't articulate.

'As some wise woman recently said, we've got the perfect backdrop, and then there's the music...and us...'

Placing her shoe in his jacket pocket, where it dangled ludicrously, he didn't wait, hauling her into his arms, holding her tight.

The sax had been joined by guitar, double bass, piano, drums, melding into a smooth jazz number washing over them, surrounding them in rhythm and sync and magic.

'I love how you move,' she said, her head resting on his chest, her arms locked tight around his waist.

'Wait 'til you see my tango and foxtrot.'

He had to make light of her admiration, had to lighten the mood before he blurted out his true feelings right here.

It was too soon for that—too soon to acknowledge anything other than they were good together out of the office.

'You're just full of surprises.'

She pulled back to look up at him, her eyes wide, her lips parted as her tongue flicked out to dampen them, that tiny innocuous gesture surprising him.

She was as overwhelmed by all this as he was, and the fact his confident, sassy Starr was probably just as nervous made him feel better.

'Bet I can show you a few more surprises.'

His exaggerated wink had the desired effect and she laughed, slapped him playfully on the chest.

'In that case, why don't you come back to the bungalow and I'll show you my tap shoes.'

'Is that the same as asking me up for *coffee?*'

'Uh-huh.'

Her hand slid downwards, a slow, erotic trail towards the waistband of his trousers, where her fingertips lingered, dipped, teased. He groaned, snagged her hand.

'Come on. I have a sudden hankering to see your whole damn shoe collection.'

They laughed as she slipped off the other shoe, slid her

hand into his and all but dragged him along the beach back towards the cart, her feet flying, his stumbling to keep up.

Starr cranked her eyes open, her mouth relaxing into a smile when the first thing she saw was Callum propped on his elbow by her side, sleepy and dishevelled and adorably ruffled.

'What are you thinking?' she asked.

His gaze swept over her, intent, lingering, and she shivered at the passing shadow clouding his eyes.

'That tonight far surpassed my expectations.'

'How so?'

'You.' He touched her bare shoulder, his fingertip skating across her skin, raising goosebumps. 'Us.'

Us.

One tiny little word, one tiny little syllable that said so much.

After their week on the island they needed to have this talk. But something in his sombre expression made her heart clench in fear.

'So there's an us now?'

'What do you think?'

Increasingly uncomfortable beneath his penetrating stare, she dropped her gaze, settled for fiddling with the sheets, pleating them into nervous rows.

Should she tell him the truth?

That she'd fallen head over heels, yet was petrified he'd morph back into an uptight, buttoned-up boss when they headed back to Melbourne?

That she felt as if she was holding her heart in the

palm of her hand, offering it to him each time she opened up to him, only to have him pat it patronisingly and push it back at her?

That allowing herself to feel like this about him, after what she'd been through, frightened her as much as the thought of losing him, losing everything?

'If we're going to make this work you need to be honest with me.'

Her hands shook beneath the sheets, her fingers digging into the thousand-count thread, her skin clammy at the thought of laying her heart on the line when she had no idea how he really felt.

But she had to do this—had to know before all the supposition and worry drove her insane.

She took a deep breath, exhaled through pursed lips. 'I like you. A lot. But you confuse the heck out of me. You've been like a different guy this last week, and I have no idea if it's going to last or if we're living in some kind of fantasy here on the island.'

Silence greeted her blurted proclamation and she reluctantly looked up, expecting to see curiosity at best, derision at worst.

When her wary gaze collided with his, what she saw took her breath away.

An emotion that went beyond understanding or compassion or caring.

Uh-uh—what she saw in the drowning depths of his beautiful brown eyes was love.

A love she'd dreamed about since she'd never got enough from her flaky parents.

A love she'd craved and thought she'd found with Sergio.

A love she could only dream about having with a man as wonderful as Callum.

'Who are you, Callum Cartwright?' she whispered, wanting to fling herself into his arms but needing her question answered.

From the moment they'd moved beyond a fling she'd been dying to know more. Heck, she'd been dying to know everything about him.

'I'm a guy who's crazy about you.'

He smoothed her hair, her back, hauling her across the bed and into his arms, hugging her until she could barely breathe.

When he finally released her she wriggled back, watched him struggle with something before finally meeting her curious gaze.

'I'm also a guy who doesn't do relationships.'

'Oh.'

'Until now.'

He strummed her back, his fingers moving absent-mindedly as she held her breath, filled with elation that he wanted more, yet half expecting a big 'but' to accompany his declaration.

'I haven't had time for a relationship—no interest in one, really. Too busy building the business.'

'But it practically runs itself it's so successful. Thanks to you.'

He paused, his expression solemn. 'Not just me.'

She shook her head, confused. 'I don't get it.'

Swiping a hand across his face, he closed his eyes, snapping them open as she reached out in concern. The bleakness in their dark depths pierced her soul.

'I took over from my older brother Archie when he died.'

'I'm sorry. How old were you?'

'Nineteen.'

'Heck, that must've been tough.'

He nodded, pain contorting his features. 'It was my fault.'

Wariness stole through her. 'What do you mean?'

'I'd been out with the boys. We were drinking, carousing, making nuisances of ourselves. The cops picked us up for being drunk and disorderly, threw us in the lock-up to teach us a lesson more than anything.' His mouth twisted, his agony obvious. 'I called Archie, like I always did. He was killed in a car accident on the way to the jail.'

Her heart broke at the raw emotion on his face, and she reached up, smoothed his cheek.

'Accidents happen. You can't control them.'

In a blinding flash she realised what was behind his obsessive drive, his absolute focus on business.

'You feel guilty…'

Only when his eyes widened and his mouth dropped open did she realise she'd spoken aloud, and mentally kicked herself for being so insensitive.

'I'm sorry. I didn't mean to—'

He placed a finger over her lips. 'Shh…don't apologise. You're right.'

He shook his head. 'Archie was the best damn CEO Cartwrights ever had, and I've spent my life trying to make up for it, to make the corporation the best as he would've wanted.'

'Do you have any other family?'

Shutters slammed down, obliterating all expression. 'My younger brother Rhys coped with his grief by running away, and my folks are based in London now.'

'You don't see them?'

'Dad's still active in the business overseas. We're not close.'

'Your mum? Rhys?'

'Mum blames me for Archie's death. We haven't spoken since. Rhys rings occasionally.'

Darn it, she'd wanted to know what made Callum tick, and now she had her answers. Problem was, she'd opened an emotional wound she had no hope of cauterising.

Unless she could distract him…

'My folks died a while back, but we weren't close. They were pretty flaky. Actors. Followed auditions on a whim, dragged me all over the country.'

'You hated it?'

'Oh, yeah, it was the pits. All I ever wanted was a home, somewhere I could belong and have real friends, know that when I got home every night I could relax without fear of finding my suitcase packed and having to move.'

He snapped his fingers. '*That's* why you love the cottage so much?'

She nodded. 'I thought I'd found a special home in

Sydney, with my ex. I worked hard, paid the rent, trusted him to build a dream of a new dance company for the both of us. And he tore it down.'

Callum's pithy curse made her smile.

'Yeah, he was full of that too, and I believed every word that tripped out of his lying mouth. He said he loved me. He said he'd make me the star of our own company. He said if I paid the rent on the apartment he'd use his money to start up the company…'

'And?'

He touched her arm, gentle, caring, and she swallowed the bitterness lodged like a fishbone in her throat.

'He cheated on me, threatened to have me fired if I walked out on him, and when I did, asking him for half the rent I'd paid over the years, he made true on his threat.'

'That money was yours—'

'Technically we were in a de facto relationship, so half that money was mine. But I didn't want to be dragged through the courts, and that's what he would've done. He still had his savings. I had nothing. It just wasn't worth it.'

'That bastard took advantage of you. Let me—'

'No.'

She held up her hand, wanting to put this in the past once and for all.

'I left Sydney to escape all that. The dance world is small. Sergio knows all the heavyweights in the industry. I can't risk my career over the jerk, no matter how much I'd like to.'

'Surely there's something you can do? Have you sought legal advice? Have you—?'

'Stop! You're being bossy again.'

He ran a hand over his face, erased his sheepish expression.

'Force of habit. Sorry.'

She loved a man who could apologise. More to the point, she loved *this* man. Every strong, controlling inch of him.

'Sydney is in the past. When I started working with you and moved into the cottage I finally felt safe again, for the first time in ages.'

'You can stay as long as you like…'

Her warning glance did the trick and he clamped his lips shut.

'It's not the cottage,' she said.

Confusion creased his brow into a frown, and as he opened his mouth to respond she rushed on.

'It's you. You're the one that makes me feel secure. Not the job, not the cottage. You.'

She shimmied forward, took hold of his hands, betting his stunned expression would only intensify when she continued.

'When I first arrived in Melbourne I realised I'd never loved Sergio. I fell in love with our lifestyle—knowing the same people, moving in the same social circles, working together, living together. It was what I thought I'd always wanted.'

Placing her hands on his chest, she slid them upwards, interlocking behind his neck.

''Til I met you.'

He crushed her to him, his kiss gentle and tender.

'I'm in love with you,' he blurted, dazed, a man shaken to his very core.

'Same here.'

Her goofy grin matched his as they stared at each other in wonder, her heart expanding with so much emotion she thought it would burst.

'So where do we go from here?'

Tipping her chin up, he brushed her bottom lip with his thumb.

'Think you can handle a full-blown relationship?'

'I can handle anything you care to dish out.'

'That's why I wanted tonight to be special. Make this thing between us real.'

Sliding her hand along his thigh, over his hip, scrunching the sheet in her fist and tugging it lower until it barely covered his impressive erection tenting the cotton, she smiled the self-satisfied smile of a woman who had it all. And was about to get some more.

'Feels pretty real to me.'

Her fingertips inched under the sheet, grazed his erection. She savoured her power over him when his head fell back and he moaned loudly.

'Still does.'

With a growl, he stilled her hand and flipped her onto her back, nuzzling her neck until she whimpered.

'Yep, very real,' he murmured, kissing his way down her neck, along her jaw, biting the edge of her robe between his teeth and dragging it until her breast popped free.

'All real…'

He repeated the same on the other side, raising himself over her when her chest was exposed, his reverent expression filling her with desire and heat and need.

'Love me.' She reached for his face, pulled it down.

Her heart swelled when he whispered, 'My pleasure…' a moment before his lips touched hers.

CHAPTER FOURTEEN

'THAT'S the seventh morning in a row I've seen your dishy man leave here at the crack of dawn to head over to the conference room.'

Katja, one of the resort's maids, stood alongside Starr and watched Callum strut towards the cart. If the older woman had any sense her eyes would be riveted to his butt, exactly as hers were.

Starr sighed, leaned against the doorjamb, raising her hand in a jaunty wave as he reached the cart, nodded at her, his sizzling smile filled with promise.

Opening up to Callum had surpassed her wildest expectations. And now she knew he loved her, knew where this relationship was heading—into the happily-ever-after she'd always dreamed about—she could have walked on water back to the mainland.

'Must be nice, working for a guy like that and maintaining a relationship away from work too.'

Katja's wistful sigh as Callum steered away from the kerb and tooted his horn didn't capture her attention half as much as the maid's comment.

They'd practically lived together ever since she'd started working for him. She'd spent every waking minute with him, and now most of her nights too.

Was the speed of their relationship a by-product of proximity? And, if so, what would happen when she found the dance job she craved?

Would Callum revert to his trusty business, continue to assuage his guilt, leaving no room in his life for her?

Icy dread trickled through her veins at the thought, freezing every ounce of confidence he'd restored with his declaration.

He'd said he loved her. It should be enough.

But she'd heard that vow before—empty words, used to cajole and convince and get what the guy wanted.

Callum wasn't like that. She was just letting her old stupid insecurities taint what they had.

Oblivious to her misgivings, Katja prattled on. 'He's a keeper, that one. You'll never want for anything as long as you're with him. Lucky you.'

Yeah, lucky me, she thought, hating that she'd allowed doubts to creep in to their relationship so early—and today of all days, when she'd been on a high after their deep and meaningful last night.

'Anyway, enough babbling from me. I'll clean your bungalow and be out in a jiffy.'

'Okay.'

As she glanced at her watch, wondering how much time she had before meeting Callum at the conference room to start work, her gaze fell on their beach towels, her bikini.

A glimmer of an idea shimmered into her consciousness—an idea that would banish her doubts, at
least for today.

Now all she had to do was convince her boss to go
for it.

Callum dropped his towel at the pool edge, stretched
and took a deep breath, surveying the lush garden on this
spectacular morning.

Everything looked brighter: the freshly mown grass
and trimmed hedges were greener, the riot of bougain-
villea a dazzling rainbow, the water sparkled a crystal-
clear aqua.

Feeling foolish, he dropped his arms, but couldn't
wipe the goofy grin off his face.

He knew why this morning was so spectacular, and
it had little to do with the weather and everything to do
with one gorgeous, sassy, hot woman who had convinced him to play hooky for the first time in his career
after another sizzling hour of memorable early-
morning sex.

They were incredible in bed together, having the kind
of sex he'd heard discussed in the gym locker room.
He'd always assumed it was big boys bragging about
fictitious encounters. But it was more than that. They
had a connection, a real one, and the longer he spent in
her ravishing company the harder he fell.

Their declarations last night should have sent him
running for the next business conference in Greenland.
Instead, he was content for the first time since Archie's

death, a part of him coming alive in a way he'd never thought possible.

Sharing his innermost thoughts with her, especially regarding his guilt associated with Archie's death, was tantamount to making a lifetime commitment.

He'd never opened up to anyone about his feelings, and discussing it with her had been strangely cathartic.

What they had was real. Scary, but real.

But his fear had receded little by little, eroded by her warmth and passion and genuine spontaneity.

With a rueful shake of his head he dived into the water, hoping a few laps would clear his head of love-struck musings.

He'd barely finished his third lap when a shadow dappled the shallow end, and he surfaced to find his dream woman wearing a red scrap of material passing as a bikini.

'That's new.'

'You like?'

'Hell, yeah.'

He reached for her, unprepared for the swift, hard shove in the middle of his chest that had him teetering on the edge of the step for a second before plunging backwards into the water.

He spluttered to the surface to find her laughing, her eyes sparkling with mischief, and his heart turned over with how much he loved this woman.

'You shouldn't have done that.'

Her mouth curved into a teasing smile. 'Why? What are you going to do about it?'

'This.'

Before she could blink he'd dived underwater, tugged her legs, bringing her under with him.

They thrashed together to the surface, her laughter the sweetest sound he'd ever heard as she wrapped her legs around his waist, hooked her hands behind his neck.

'So you're a big tough guy now, huh?'

'Actually, I'm turning into a big softie around you.' He faked a frown. 'But, shh…don't tell anyone. Terrible for my reputation and bad for business.'

Her smile faded and she nibbled on her bottom lip.

'Hey, what did I say?'

She wrinkled her nose. 'I don't know if I should tell you this and spoil our last day.'

'Tell me what?'

When her lips clamped shut he tickled her, and she sighed.

'As I was leaving the bungalow a call came through. Some guy saying it was urgent, but he wouldn't leave his name or a message.'

His brain leaped to a host of possibilities before he deliberately calmed. He hadn't had a day off in years, and he wanted to spend this last day on the island with her.

'Although…' All the cheek had drained out of her and she shrugged. 'He did say something like "Get that damn stand-in to ring me."'

Hell.

Only one person would say something like that.

And the fact dear old dad was calling him on the eve of one of Cartwright's biggest deals sent foreboding stabbing through him.

'Starr, I'm sorry. I have to—'

'Go.'

She sighed, slithered out of his arms. 'I figured you would if I told you.'

'You did the right thing.'

Climbing the ladder, he hoisted himself out of the pool, grabbed his towel, tied it around his waist, chilled by more than a sudden gust of wind as he contemplated what Frank Cartwright could possibly want.

'Do you need me for anything?'

He shook his head, his gaze zeroing in on her cleavage as she propped herself on her forearms on the pool's edge, temptingly buxom.

Jeez, what was wrong with him? Even at a time like this, when faced with a possible problem, he couldn't get his mind off sex with Starr.

'I'll see you later.'

'Call me if you need anything.'

He raised a hand in farewell. The only thing he needed for a phone call with his father was a thick skin—something he'd honed to great effect since his teenage years, when Frank had viewed him as the screw-up of his boys. His opinion had never changed, despite him busting a gut to make up for Archie's death all these years.

Barging into the bungalow, Callum slung his beach towel over the back of a chair and reached for his mobile.

The sooner he got this over with, the sooner he could return to Starr.

Punching in a number from memory storage, he waited, not surprised when Frank answered on the second ring. Patience wasn't a virtue Frank Cartwright cultivated.

'Where the hell have you been?'

No polite greeting, as usual, which only made him want to reinforce normal phone etiquette more.

'Hi, Dad. I'm good. You?'

He'd learned a long time ago to keep his cool, not to lose control around his father. It only fuelled his rage, gave him more ammunition to belittle him with.

'This merger is about to go pear-shaped and you want to exchange pleasantries? What the hell is wrong with you?'

Mention of the merger had him snapping to attention, and he clutched the phone to his ear.

Last he knew, everything was signed, sealed and delivered. It was the reason he'd taken today off—that and the fact he couldn't say no to his beautiful girlfriend.

'The merger is fine.'

'Bull! I've fielded five phone calls in the last half-hour from execs who can't get hold of you and are panicking. What's the deal?'

'Everything is fine—'

'Aren't you listening to a word I've said? The bloody deal's off! They've invoked the cooling-off period.'

Stunned, Callum collapsed onto the nearest chair. 'But I handled it personally. They were—'

'Fishing for a better offer—and they've found it, dammit!'

He held the phone away from his ear as Frank continued to bellow.

'You've screwed up!'

Disgust crawled across his skin as he rubbed the back of his neck. The deal falling through had sent his blood pressure skyrocketing, but not as much as his father's lack of confidence in him.

'Go ahead, Dad, why don't you say it?' Regret, heavy and thick, roiled in his gut. 'I screwed up. *Again*.'

Frank paused, before spitting out, 'You said it.'

He should be used to this by now—his father's total disdain for him as a person, as a son—but it still hurt as much now as it always had.

'There's nothing else I can do to make up for Archie's death, Dad. He's gone and I'm doing my best to—'

'Don't you *dare* bring your brother into this! He's gone, thanks to you.'

The venom in Frank's tone was nothing new, and at that moment Callum realised something.

Nothing he said or did would ever be enough for his dad.

He was done trying to apologise for Archie's death, done trying to make amends.

Everything he did at Cartwrights from now on in would be for him, for Rhys, for the memory of a brother he'd give anything to have back in his life.

Frank could go jump.

'I'll salvage what I can from the deal.'

Which was more than he could say for their relationship.

Frank snorted his contempt. 'Yeah, good luck with that.'

'Bye, Dad.'

He hung up on the man who'd never been a father to him, a man who wouldn't know the meaning of the word. Flinging the phone at the far wall gave him little satisfaction.

Fury pumped through his veins as he stalked the room, clenching his fists, needing an outlet for his rage.

As a teen, he'd dealt with his father and mother's indifference by rebelling, doing anything and everything to get their attention.

But they hadn't given a damn—had been too busy playing First Couple in Australia's financial circles, living up to their business mogul reputations to bother about him or Rhys.

Archie had been the golden child, the chosen one, the eldest, who'd fallen into line and done exactly what Frank and Maureen wanted. They'd adored him, focussed all their energies on their first-born, and had had nothing left to give to their other sons.

It had made it all the easier for him—shirking responsibility, doing exactly as he pleased.

Until the night Archie died—a night none of them had ever recovered from.

'Damn it!'

He punched his fist into the wall, barely registering the pain, and Starr chose that moment to waltz in the door.

'Hey! Are you okay?'

She rushed towards him, opened her arms, and he

stepped back, held up his hands to ward her off. He needed space right now, needed to calm down, gather his thoughts and get back to work to salvage what he could from the botched deal.

Hating the hurt in her eyes, he crossed to the other side of the bungalow, grabbed his suit, shirt and tie before heading for the bathroom.

'Callum. Talk to me.'

He whirled on her, anger making him crazy.

'And tell you what? That by taking the day off today I've lost the company billions?'

Her mouth sagged before she snapped it shut. 'I thought the deal was done.'

'You thought wrong.'

She flinched at his outburst, and while his brain knew she didn't deserve to bear the brunt of his anger he was running on pure emotion now—something he never did.

'Is it salvageable?'

Her calm tone riled him further. He wanted her to rant and rave at him for being such an idiot, give him an opportunity to really let fly.

'Anything I can do?'

'Yeah, you can leave me the hell alone.'

In a flash her calmness vanished, and her chest heaved, her hair bristled like a golden Statue of Liberty, her eyes sparked indigo fire, and all he could think was how gorgeous she looked and how much he'd like to take her up against the nearest wall.

'Are you implying this is my fault?'

Her voice, deadly calm, screeched across his nerves

like nails down a blackboard, and realisation slammed into him full force.

He *did* blame her. His anger was equally directed at his dad, the injustice of losing Archie, and at her, for distracting him from what he did best. Staying in control, staying on top.

If she walked away now, gave him a chance to cool down, he might have a chance of not saying something he'd regret.

Instead her mouth twisted, her eyes filled with betrayal, and the knowledge he'd hurt her kicked him in the guts.

This was why he didn't do involvement. Falling for someone, caring what they thought, robbed him of his detachment, robbed him of control.

He hated feeling like this, had vowed after the last time it would never happen again.

Only one thing to do: push her away before he lost it completely and did long-term damage to the company that meant everything to him.

Folding his arms, he leaned against the bathroom door and nodded.

'I'm not implying anything. I'm stating a fact.'

'What the—?'

'You convinced me to play hooky today. You, with your constant smiles and upbeat peppiness and glass half-full crap.' He jabbed a finger in her direction, his anger spilling out in a torrent. '*This* is why I don't do involvement. It ruins concentration, ruins companies. You—'

'Stop right there.'

Tears filled her eyes, turning them a luminous blue, and something broke inside him.

What had he done?

'Starr—'

'No!'

She blinked, the teardrops clinging to the ends of her lashes scattering like delicate rain before she shook her head.

'Don't say another word.'

Regret, anguish, loss, contorted her features as she backed away a few steps, before turning and making a run for the door.

He could have called out to her.

Dashed after her.

Implored her to listen.

He did none of those things.

Turning away, he stepped into the bathroom and slammed the door.

On the best thing that ever happened to him.

CHAPTER FIFTEEN

STARR SPRINTED TO catch the last tram, ignoring the curious looks from passengers as she tripped up the steps and collapsed onto the nearest empty seat.

She hugged her bag close, comforted by its contents: her favourite audition outfit. Fluoro orange legwarmers, her oldest dance shoes, her lucky charm butterfly bracelet.

'You've got the job, Miss Merriday. Welcome to Studio Bolero.'

The phrase still echoed through her head, had kept tempo with her feet as she'd run down the street to the tram stop. She should be ecstatic, should have twirled and jigged and allemanded her way onto the tram.

Instead she slunk into her seat, clutched her bag tight and tried to ignore the constant pain in her chest.

Damn Callum Cartwright for taking the gloss off her first dance job in Melbourne.

And damn him for breaking her heart.

She'd known it was all too good to be true: the cottage, the job, the incredible guy. All a mirage that had vanished as quickly as his supposed love for her.

Love? What a crock.

She should be thankful. When she'd taken the first flight out of Hayman Island, e-mailed him her resignation, it had taken her a day to do what she should have done the moment she landed in Melbourne.

Chase down more leads. Not settle for rejection. Push her way into auditions she knew she could nail, given half a chance.

And now she could move out of Kit's uni friend's halfway house again, and into a tiny apartment over the Studio Bolero.

She'd be gone before he returned—just the way she wanted.

She couldn't face him. Not without hurling something at him. Not without verbally abusing him.

Her fingers flexed, digging into her straw bag, and her entire body was taut with tension.

She could kill him for what he'd done to her, to them, but that part of her life was over, finished. She had to get used to it.

This was what she wanted. Dance was her life.

The moment she'd stepped onto the old stage at the studio, surrounded by bright lights shielding the yawning seats in front of her, with dust motes from the heavy crimson velvet curtains shimmering under the spotlight, the distinctive smell of greasepaint lingering in the air, a sense of coming home had descended over her—a sense of belonging she found nowhere but in dance.

Then the music had started, a familiar tune from

Fame sending a chill down her spine as she'd waited for the first kicked-up beat before spinning into her routine.

It came naturally now—the spins, the twirls, the lunges, the dramatic leap and roll at the end.

She'd done the entire audition by rote, eyes closed, feeling the music, feeling the beat, feeling alive.

No matter what she faced, dance was the one constant in her life. It had never let her down—unlike her poor choice in men.

'Miss?'

Her eyes snapped open to find the conductor looming over her, and she flashed her ticket, sneaked a quick glance out of the window, grateful her stop was coming up.

The sooner she packed her backpack and headed back to Bolero, the sooner she could unwind. She needed a long, hot bath, an extra-strength hot chocolate and a night watching *Sex and the City* re-runs to clear her head.

She was doing the right thing.

Her life was back on track.

Then why did she still feel seriously derailed?

'Have you heard from Dad?'

Callum quit staring into his coffee mug, glared at the phone where he had Rhys on loud speaker. 'Don't tell me. He rang you to sing my praises.'

'You and me both, bro. Apparently I'm a disgrace to the Cartwright name. A good-for-nothing lout squandering my life.'

Callum winced. 'Nice.'

'The old man's in top form. So what's new?'

Callum leaned back, locked hands behind his head. 'He rang me while I was on Hayman Island. Apparently taking my first day off in fourteen years resulted in the company losing a lucrative merger.'

Rhys swore. 'Are you serious? Tell me you didn't buy into his aggressive bull.'

His relationship with Starr was in tatters, he couldn't concentrate on business, and the corporation had suffered a sizeable loss the last financial quarter, discounting the botched merger.

Serious? He was a walking disaster.

'Cal? What did you do?'

Rhys paused, astute, assessing, and though they'd never been close Callum had a burning need to unburden to someone before he burst.

'I stuffed up.

'With the deal?'

'And the rest.'

Rhys whistled, long and low. 'You mucked up things with that hot PA, didn't you?'

'That's putting it mildly.'

No matter how hard he tried to concentrate on business, he couldn't wipe the image of her shattered expression, her tears, as he'd deliberately pushed her away because of his own failure.

The memory ate at him, leaving a residual ache in the vicinity of his heart.

He didn't want to have this conversation, didn't want to acknowledge that with every second without Starr he died a little inside.

'Lovers' tiff?'

The instant rebuttal died on his lips as he heard the genuine concern in Rhys' voice.

'It's over.'

'What happened?'

'I blamed her. She distracted me. I played hooky for the day. The deal went south.'

Rhys let fly another pithy curse. 'So you let the old man get to you. You should've run, like me, rather than get caught up in his bull.'

'I'm not doing this for him.'

Rhys sighed. 'I know, bro, you're doing it for Archie. But how long are you going to live your life like this? You do nothing but work. You don't have fun any more. You're closed off to everyone. You—'

'You're not helping.'

'Just saying it as it is.'

The annoying thing was, Rhys was right. The night Archie had died he'd turned his back on everything he'd ever enjoyed.

No more scuba-diving, parachuting, hang-gliding.

No more parties, dating, drinking.

He'd shut himself off physically, emotionally, and it had taken a wild, sassy dancer with long legs to revive him.

And what had he done?

Shoved her away as hard as he could.

'Do you care about her?'

He stood, started pacing his office, sending the phone a ferocious glare.

'Damn straight I do.'

'Then start grovelling.'

Rhys chuckled, though he found nothing about this situation remotely funny. He needed to swallow a bottle of antacids to douse the anxiety burning him up inside.

'Come on bro, get off your moral high horse, stop convincing yourself you're better off without her, and go apologise before it's too late.'

'So says the relationship expert.'

'Hey, when was *your* last relationship, Romeo?'

'When was yours?'

Rhys laughed, and Callum managed a wry grin. They never talked like this. He'd been focussed on business, and Rhys had flung himself into his adventurous life overseas. It had been this way for years.

Then it hit him.

While he'd been caught up in Cartwrights, caught up in making up for his mistakes, his younger brother had grown into a man: a decent man. A man who cared enough to ring a brother who rarely returned the sentiment, a man who cared enough to offer advice, a man who just plain listened.

All the good intentions in the world wouldn't make Archie come back, and he needed to start building bridges with the one brother he had left.

'I'm sorry I've ignored you all these years.'

Rhys paused, cleared his throat, his voice strangely husky when he spoke. 'Where is my brother and what have you done with him?'

'Quit it.'

'Seriously, bro. I've never heard you so emotional. You don't do the broken heart thing well.'

'Shut up and listen—'

'It's okay, I get it. We were devastated over Archie. We handled it in different ways—'

'It's more than that—'

'You've got plenty of time to pull the big brother routine on me. Who knows? Maybe I'll visit Melbourne soon and we can catch up over a few beers? But right now you need to concentrate on getting your life back on track. I know where I'm going. Do you?'

He knew.

He just didn't know what was scarier: the journey or the destination.

Starr wriggled out of her legwarmers and tossed them next to her tap shoes as her mobile rang.

She hated how her heart danced with expectation as she glanced at the caller ID, only to plummet when she registered Kit.

What kind of masochist wanted to talk to a guy who'd banished her from his life without flinching?

Plopping onto the lumpy sofa, she hit the answer button, wriggling to find a comfortable spot that didn't involve dodgy sagging, loaded springs. This studio apartment was a godsend, but built for comfort it wasn't.

'Hey Kitty-Kat. Long time, no hear.'

'Are you insane? I called you yesterday.'

As she glanced around the tiny studio apartment—and she used the word *apartment* very loosely—with its shabby, threadbare chairs, pocked floorboards, dingy one-window lighting and total lack of charm, it seemed like a lifetime since she'd heard from her friend.

Her new job might be fabulous, but her new digs were far from it. Every time she closed her eyes she could envisage the cottage: bright yellow walls, gleaming golden floorboards, comfy cushions piled high on squishy sofas, and she wished she could grab her bags, call a cab and head back to Toorak.

'How's the job working out?'

Glancing at the flyer advertising the upcoming season of *Chicago,* she knew things weren't all bad.

'It's great. The cast is talented…'

'Usual bitchiness?'

'Yeah, and the girls aren't too welcoming either.'

Kit's laughter was as melodious and tuneful as her renowned singing on stage.

'You'll be fine. I've seen you handle worse.'

The crackling of a chocolate bar being opened tore down the line, followed by loud munching. 'Speaking of handling anything—heard from Cal-Pal?'

'As if.'

It had been two days since she'd vacated the cottage and moved in here—forty-eight long, agonising hours during which she had checked her mobile for messages between rehearsals, and glanced at her watch wondering what he was doing, wishing he would arrive on her doorstep and say it had all been some big mistake.

Crazy, because if he did she'd tell him where to

shove his apology, but she hadn't expected to miss him this much.

Yeah, right, and she'd be starring on Broadway next week.

'But who cares, right?'

Kit's *faux*-innocence brought a reluctant smile to her face. While she might not have told her friend everything about her relationship with the commanding CEO, Kit was astute enough to read between the lines.

'It's better this way.'

The decibel of Kit's inelegant snort had her edging the phone away from her ear.

'Better for whom? This guy has been good for you. After that slime-bag Sergio—'

'Can we please not mention his name? It gives me hives.'

'You sounded happy again, really happy, and it couldn't have been the boring office job, holed up with Mr CEO twenty-four-seven, so that means you two must've done the horizontal cha-cha and—'

'Think I can get a word in here?'

'Only if you're lucky.'

Kit's chuckles warmed her, as they always did. Her friend was one of very few people she trusted. So why the reluctance to confide? Why hold back when she'd blurted every minute detail of her relationship with Sergio?

Deep down, she knew.

How could she vocalise even half of what she was feeling, the depth of her love, when she didn't want to acknowledge it let alone analyse it?

She missed Callum.

Missed seeing him sleep-tousled and slightly grumpy in the morning before his double-shot espresso.

Missed casting surreptitious peeks at him while he handled a few million dollars like a practised circus juggler.

Missed his rare but brilliant smiles, his frequent praise, his passion in and out of the bedroom…

'So what really happened between you two?'

Where should she start?

The fact that she hadn't been able to keep her hands off him from the first week she'd started working for him?

The fact she'd fallen in love with him so quickly her head still spun?

The fact that it would take her a lifetime to get over him?

She couldn't say any of those things, so she settled for an excuse.

'I need my space. I found the job I should've got in the first place and moved out. Working and living-in became too cosy.'

'Bull. Cosy's what you want.'

Starr tensed, her breathing accelerating at Kit's unsaid words: *some place safe, someone to make you feel safe.*

Yes, she wanted that. It was the main reason she'd hung around with Sergio long after the spark in their relationship had died. She wanted that with every breath in her body. But Callum wasn't the guy she'd thought he was, couldn't give her what she wanted, and it still hurt. Boy, did it hurt.

'That job was an interim, you know that.'

'And Mr CEO? Was he just a stop-gap too? Or should I call him Rebound Guy and be done with it?'

'He wasn't a rebound!'

'My, my, aren't we defensive?'

Starr rolled her shoulders, kinked her neck from side to side, tried to relax.

She should know Kit by now—know her penchant for winding her up, for teasing the truth out of her by any means. But this time her lips were staying sealed.

'Kit?'

'Hmm?'

'I've got to get back to rehearsal.'

Another snort. 'You've made an art form out of running away.'

Staring at the glossy *Chicago* brochure in her hand, she knew she'd made the right career move in leaving Sydney, even if she'd been bolting rather than running from her past.

'Melbourne suits me. You'd see for yourself if you ever visited.'

'Three more months, babe, and I'm there.'

'I'll hold you to that.'

'And, hun?'

'Yeah?'

'Maybe my visit will coincide with your nuptials?'

Cackling at the curse Starr let fly, Kit hung up before she could respond, leaving her contemplating a scenario so far from comprehension it belonged right up there with dreams of winning a Tony award or starring along-side Hugh Jackman in *The Boy from OZ*.

Never going to happen.

Not that she hadn't dreamed about tying herself to Callum for life on the island. She had tied herself up into deliciously anticipatory knots at the thought.

But, as she knew better than anyone, her romantic dreams had turned to nightmares.

CHAPTER SIXTEEN

AFTER making a few discreet phone calls, Callum finally had the information he required.

His first instinct was to high-tail it to Starr's new address as fast as humanly possible and do what he had to do.

But if they were to have any kind of future he had some unfinished business to take care of first.

Wiping his sweaty palm along his trousers, he picked up the phone, dialled, knowing he should have done this a long time ago.

'Frank Cartwright.'

'Dad, it's me.'

'Hope you've got some good news for me after that merger fiasco.'

The words *shove it* prodded, begged to be said, but he needed to have this conversation for his peace of mind so he swallowed them.

'This isn't about business.'

'Then what? I don't have time to make chit-chat—'

'We need to talk about Archie.'

Frank swore. The curse was nothing he hadn't heard

a hundred times growing up, when he'd never lived up to expectations in his father's eyes.

'Just leave it the hell alone.'

Propping himself on the side of his desk, Callum rubbed his chest where a constant ache resided: for the loss of the brother he'd adored, the loss of his youth and, more recently, the loss of the woman who was everything to him.

'No. You don't have to say a damn thing, just listen.' Anticipating Frank's comeback, he added, 'And don't think about hanging up. If you do, I'll quit.'

It wasn't an idle threat. If his father didn't give him the opportunity to have his say after all these years, he'd walk.

'What's all this about?'

Frank's gruff tone was underlined with steel, but at least he'd conceded.

'I'm done trying to make up for Archie's accident. You don't give a hoot what I've done for the company, how much I've put in. The only time I ever hear from you is to berate me. Something I've put up with through my own guilt, but not any more.'

'What are you going to do?'

His father's sneer rolled off him. The condescending bitterness was something he'd lived with almost all his life.

'Tell you how it is.'

He rubbed the bridge of his nose, hoping to stave off the headache building.

'I didn't ask for this job, didn't want it. The only reason I'm at Cartwright is to preserve Archie's memory. You blame me? No more than I blame myself—and being a part of your precious company reinforces that guilt every single day.'

He took a deep breath and continued, needing to get this off his chest before it festered any longer.

'It doesn't matter that you were so busy building your almighty business you ignored Rhys and me growing up. It doesn't matter that nothing I did or said got your attention. And it sure as hell doesn't matter that I've worked my ass off for the last fourteen years, giving two hundred percent in the hope you'd cut me some slack.'

Standing, he strode across his office, looked out of the window. Glimpsing the cottage through the immaculately trimmed trees, he was spurred on to finish this once and for all.

'What does matter is how I'm going to run things from now on. No more working around the clock for your conference calls from London. No more working fifty-two weeks a year. And no more calls like the one on Hayman Island. From now, I do this my way.'

A small part of him wished for an apology, some small semblance of affection, any indication that his father had once loved him, had *ever* loved him.

But he'd given up on futile dreams a long time ago, the night he'd held Archie's hand in hospital as he'd taken his last breath and wished he could take it all back, so he knew Frank would never acknowledge him in the way he'd always wanted.

'Just keep those profit margins up,' Frank growled, his tone devoid of any sentiment bar avarice.

'That's all you have to say?'

'Goodbye, son.'

As the dial tone hummed in his ear, he stared at the phone, disbelief warring with relief.

He'd said his piece.

He was about to instigate major changes in his life—all for the better.

But what shocked him the most was Frank calling him 'son' for the first time ever.

He might not have received the recognition he wanted, the recognition he deserved, but from the narcissistic world of Frank Cartwright, Callum hearing him acknowledge he had another son was a start.

Maybe there was hope for the old reprobate yet.

Starr gritted her teeth and forced a smile for the umpteenth time that evening, wishing she'd never agreed to take this jazz ballet class.

Standing in for a sick teacher was one thing. Having to kick her legs and swing her arms and look happy about it in front of a bunch of teenagers was another.

What was it with the kids of today? They were taller and gutsier and far more astute than she'd ever been at that age. Fifteen going on fifty, the lot of 'em, and if she had to field one more smart-ass question she'd make them shimmy across the splintered floor on their pierced flat bellies.

'Excuse me, miss?'

Inhaling deeply, she fixed a semblance of a pleasant smile on her face.

'Yes?'

'Is that hottie your boyfriend? Because if he isn't, we'd all like dibs.'

Yet another lousy distraction technique from this bunch of slackers who were only here because their exhausted parents needed to foist their monster teenagers on someone else for a few hours—and were willing to pay for the privilege.

They were good; she'd give them that much. They tittered and grinned and cast longing looks over her shoulder, and with an exasperated sigh she finally turned, ready to yell if they were having her on.

Her angry scream died in her throat, which was suddenly clogged with something far scarier: elation.

Quickly replaced by anger and sadness and regret.

How dared he show up here after what he'd done?

To her?

To them?

'Excuse me, girls.'

She stalked towards the door, oblivious to the twittering reaching ear-hurting decibels, determined to get rid of Callum before this day got any worse.

'Hey, sorry for showing up like this but—'

'I'm busy. Leave.'

She swivelled on her heel, faced her audience of curious onlookers, who were now goggle-eyed as well as muttering.

'No.'

His hand shot out, grabbed her arm, leaving her no option but to stop.

'Let go of me.'

Her order came out a hiss, barely audible. She hated they were doing this here, now. 'I'm working. Something *you* know all about.'

'I'm not leaving.'

Stubborn oaf.

'Fine. You'll have to join the class, then.'

Her chin thrust forward, challenging. He'd back down. No question.

As if the uptight, always-in-control Callum Cartwright would get down and jiggy with a bunch of schoolgirls.

'It's not ballroom, but what the hell?'

Stunned, she watched him shrug out of his jacket, toss it on a nearby chair, whip off his tie and shove it into his trouser pocket, and roll up his sleeves. His grin screamed triumph.

He thought he'd best her? She'd show him.

Pointing at the group of girls, who were now giggling and whispering, she said, 'You've missed the warm-up but go ahead—be my guest.'

Now was the time he'd balk, make an excuse, head for the door and wait for her to finish up. Instead, he marched straight towards the girls, introduced himself amid a flurry of blushes and giggles and sighs, then turned to face her, shoulders squared, ready for anything she could dish out and more.

He stood out among the girls, a gorgeous giant who knew his power over her, intent on wielding it. Tough. This little Lilliputian was through with being trampled on.

Clapping her hands, she waited until silence fell.

'Okay, girls—' she sent Callum a pointed smirk '—and boys, let's crank it up a little.'

The girls cheered as she hit the switch on the ancient stereo and music pulsed out of the speakers, the beat strong and loud and mesmerising.

Ignoring Callum completely, she allowed the music to infuse her, letting her body set the tempo as she let rip a string of moves that would challenge the best dancer.

The girls loved it, and to Callum's credit he did his best to keep up, that 'I'm the king of the world' grin firmly fixed in place.

And, try as she might, she couldn't help but watch him, her curious gaze drawn towards the way he moved, how in sync with the music his body was.

Oh, yeah, he had the moves, all right—and not just on the dance floor.

Her body zinged with the heat of remembrance, a heat that spread through every inch of her until her muscles cramped with it.

Dragging her gaze away from the sensuous swing of his hips, she focussed on the girls, on the steps, mixing it up a little when the music changed, setting them challenges.

As an avoidance technique, it worked. Until the music stopped and she glanced at the clock over the door. It signalled the end of class.

'Good effort, class. Let's call it a night.'

She waved at their applause, headed for her bag in the far corner of the studio, willing Callum to leave with the rest of them. Fat chance.

When the last giggle and footfall had faded she risked a glance over her shoulder, only to find him waiting patiently by the door, jacket hooked on one finger, resting on his shoulder, leaning against the wall, oh-so-casual, oh-so-divine.

Did he *have* to look so damn gorgeous when she needed to kick his cute butt out of here?

'I'm not leaving 'til we talk.'

His words carried across the room, and with a reluctant sigh she slung her bag over her shoulder and sauntered towards him.

'I kinda got that impression from the way you stuck it out for the last fifteen minutes.'

He fixed her with a determined stare—the kind of stare that meant business.

'I'm not the type of guy to walk away. From anything.'

Ignoring the traitorous beat of her heart, she shrugged. 'And here I thought you already had.'

'Wrong.' Jerking a thumb over his shoulder, he said, 'Is there somewhere private we can talk?'

She didn't want to do this—didn't want to rehash their relationship, didn't want to give him a chance to say anything that might undermine her wavering resistance, which had taken a serious hit just by seeing him again.

'There's nothing left to say, so just go—'

'Please. It's important.'

His verbal request didn't affect her half as much as the unspoken plea in his expressive eyes, and she sighed.

'Come upstairs. I'll give you five minutes, then I have to rehearse for tomorrow.'

'Sounds reasonable.'

He gestured for her to go first up the stairs.

Like hell. And have him stare at her butt all the way up? No way.

'Gentlemen first.' His grin widened at her muttered, 'And I use the term loosely,' but he bounded up the stairs like an athlete, with her trudging reluctantly behind.

The rickety old stairs weren't wide enough for two, and when she reached the top she had to squeeze past him.

A gentleman would have stepped back, given her plenty of room, but, as she'd just asserted, Callum was no gentleman.

He stood there with that smug grin on his face, his eyes darkening as she wriggled past him, carefully trying to avoid body contact, failing miserably when her breasts brushed his arm, her hips collided with his.

Gritting her teeth against the insane urge to linger, she swung her bag with particular force, somewhat mollified by his muttered curse as it connected with his elbow. She fiddled with the key and swung the door open.

'Your five minutes starts now.'

'Good. Let's start with this.'

She was wedged in the doorway, with the jamb pressed against her back, and he kissed her—hard.

A furious, desperate, no-holds-barred kiss that bombarded her senses, seared through her body, exploding like a fireball and wiping out every logical argument as to why they shouldn't be together like this always.

When she finally came to her senses it was too late.

He'd eased off, broken the kiss when it should have been her, giving him the upper hand yet again.

'That's not talking!'

She shoved him away, slammed the door and stomped to the window, feeling as thick as the ugly bricks she looked out at.

What was it about this guy that had her so befuddled with just one glance, one touch?

'Yeah, but much more fun, don't you think?'

Fixing him with a withering stare, she tapped her watch.

'Three minutes, thirty seconds. Start talking.'

'Okay.'

He draped his jacket over the back of a chair, held his hands out to her, palms up. As if she'd be stupid enough to believe he didn't hide a host of tricks up those sleeves.

'I'm sorry for overreacting on the island, for pushing you away.'

She wanted to believe him, she really did, but the memory of Sergio's duplicity had shattered her trust. Gullible might have been her middle name once, but not any more.

When she didn't say anything, glancing at her watch instead, he continued.

'I took my anger out on you when the person I was really angry at was myself, for losing concentration, losing perspective.' He shook his head, regret twisting his mouth. 'I blamed you for what happened with the deal and that was totally unfair.'

'Too right. You were an idiot, throwing away what we had.'

'You're right. The worst kind of idiot.'

She wanted to be angry at him. She wanted to fling her arms in the air, whirl around, stomp her feet. But this wasn't the time for melodrama. It was the time for truth. He owed her that much at least.

'So what was your meltdown really about? It couldn't have just been the lost merger.'

He stilled, his expression impassive, not a flicker of a muscle.

'Right again. There's more. And I know if we're to have any kind of future you need to hear the truth. All of it.'

Her heart leapt at his mention of a future, before her common sense slapped it back down.

She wasn't going to take crap from any guy ever again, remember? And right now Callum would have to get down on the floor and crawl on his belly for her to even consider taking him back.

Nonchalant, she waved her hand. 'Go on. I'm listening.'

'I haven't always been a workaholic. Before Archie died, I was the least likely guy to work in finance.' His wry grin eased some of the tension in his face. 'I had no idea what career I wanted. I was happy surfing, caving, playing hockey, doing any extreme sport I could.'

Her mouth dropped open. His words were penetrating her ears but her mind was having a hard time computing.

He chuckled at her expression. 'I was a rebel. Didn't give two hoots about anything but my next thrill. Archie was the responsible one.'

'So when he died you took over out of guilt. You've already told me.'

He shook his head, his expression open, sincere. 'That's not all of it. I rebelled because I would've done anything to get my parents—particularly my dad—to notice me. But it never worked.'

She understood all too well about unhappy teenage years feeling unwanted and ignored by parents who didn't give a fig about anyone but themselves.

It was one of the reasons she'd chosen to dance—because it had irked her folks; probably because they hadn't wanted her sharing their limelight on stage.

Though the irony hadn't been lost on her that she'd ultimately chosen a career close to theirs—had wanted to succeed on stage where they hadn't.

'Yeah, I stepped up out of guilt, but that's not the only reason. I thought by giving my all to the job I could drive away the demons, could get my dad to see I wasn't the loser he thought.' He shrugged. 'I wanted recognition, wanted him to acknowledge he still had a son left behind who'd do anything to make it up to him.'

'Oh…'

An overwhelming sadness filled her at what he'd given up, how hard he'd strived to gain his father's approval.

Didn't he know? With some people, no matter what you did or said, it was never enough.

She remembered bitterness mingling with grief at her own parents' funeral, at the fact they'd never acknowledged what she'd done with her life, no matter how many star roles or positive reviews she'd received.

'I understand.'

'Do you?'

He advanced on her, forcing her to back up until her butt hit the back of a sofa.

He stopped just short of her personal space, invading it with his potent presence anyway.

'My whole working life has revolved around making Cartwright a success. I don't take vacations. I work day and night. I haven't cared about anything other than giving my all.'

He leaned towards her, a wall of palpable heat slamming into her, bombarding her, befuddling her senses.

'Until now. Now I care about something else a hell of a lot more.'

Her tongue darted out to moisten her lips as her throat constricted with the enormity of what he was saying.

'What's that?'

'You.'

He cupped her cheek, stroked her bottom lip with his thumb, and she resisted the urge to fling herself into his arms and scream that all was forgiven.

'You're the most important thing in my life, Starr Merriday. I love you, every unpredictable, wild inch of you, and I want you in my life. Always.'

Joy fizzed through her veins like expensive champagne as she studied his face, scrutinised every minute detail, from his guileless eyes to the genuine slant of his lips.

He was telling the truth.

Truth that fissured the defensive wall she'd built around her heart after he'd hurt her, allowing half of what she felt for this incredible man to spill out, fill her, urge her to give him another chance.

'You swear I'm the most important to you? No bull?'

His lips twitched as he placed his hand over his heart.

'No bull—promise.'

'You're still CEO of Cartwright?'

'Uh-huh, but my role is undergoing some radical changes.' He held up his hand, ticked points off his fingers. 'I'm not going to work twenty-four-seven any more, I'm taking regular vacations, and *I'm* the boss, doing things my way, not to appease my father.'

'That's good.'

She tilted her head up, met his hopeful gaze.

'So what about me? Where do I fit into all this?'

His smile twinkled mischievously in his eyes.

'Like I said, you come first. Work is a distant second.'

She arched an eyebrow. 'Really?'

He chuckled. 'Really. Mind you, I'll always run things, boss people around, stay in control.'

Tracing a fingertip down her cheek, he outlined her lips, smiled at her sharp intake of breath.

'Except around you.'

He bundled her into his arms, hugged her tight, but not before she'd glimpsed genuine happiness darkening his eyes to ebony.

'I think that's what scared me the most on the island, what contributed to my meltdown—the fact I always lose control around you. You're my weakness.'

With her arms locked around his waist, her face buried in his chest, she inhaled, let him wash through

her senses, his familiarity soothing the aching, lost part
of her soul that had mourned him this last week.

Being in his arms, being near him, made her feel safe,
and there was no place in the world she'd rather be.

Safe…with him…

'Oh!'

Wrenching away, she grabbed his shirt, bunched it in
her hands, shook him slightly.

'What's wrong?'

'Me. I'm so dense!'

Amusement lit his face. 'Stubborn, maybe. Dense,
not so much.'

Releasing him, she smoothed his shirt, patted his
chest. 'Just hear me out.'

'Okay.'

'I've spent my whole life wanting security.'

'And that's a bad thing because…?'

'Just listen.'

She whacked him gently on the chest before moving
away, needing space and air and distance to clarify her
thoughts and how she'd articulate them to make him
understand.

'You know about my parents, how we moved around.
And I've already told you how you make me feel safe.
But it's more than that…'

She whirled around, clicked her fingers. 'That week
on Hayman Island was the happiest I've ever felt. Want
to know why?'

'The sex?'

She whacked him playfully on the arm. 'The intimacy

we shared. Though it was only a week, the way we talked, shared our innermost thoughts—'

He raised a dubious eyebrow '—well, most of them,' she continued. 'It was a closeness I've never had with another person.'

'Even your ex?'

She snorted. 'Living with someone, being in a relationship, doesn't guarantee intimacy.'

'I wouldn't know—being the relationship virgin I am, and all.'

His mock-bashful expression made her laugh with delight and she flung herself into his arms, wrapped her legs around his waist and held on for dear life.

'That thing you mentioned earlier?'

Trailing kisses along her neck, nuzzling behind her earlobe, he murmured, 'What thing?'

Her head fell back, and a loud moan was ripped from within as he nibbled the sensitive spot halfway between her jaw and collarbone.

'About you loving me? Wanting me in your life? Always?'

'Yeah, what about it?'

Capturing his face in her hands, she eyeballed him. 'Right back at you.'

His triumphant, ecstatic grin took years off his face, melting away the tension that had become as much a part of him as his fancy suits.

'You and me. Always,' he murmured, a second before his lips touched hers, confirming what she'd unconsciously known.

No matter how many standing ovations she received, no matter how many perfect pirouettes she performed, nothing could beat the rush of being loved by the right man.

LARGER-PRINT BOOKS!

HARLEQUIN *Presents*

PASSION
GUARANTEED
SEDUCTION

GET 2 FREE LARGER-PRINT NOVELS PLUS 2 FREE GIFTS!

YES! Please send me 2 FREE LARGER-PRINT Harlequin Presents® novels and my 2 FREE gifts (gifts are worth about $10). After receiving them, if I don't wish to receive any more books, I can return the shipping statement marked "cancel". If I don't cancel, I will receive 6 brand-new novels every month and be billed just $4.55 per book in the U.S. or $5.24 per book in Canada. That's a saving of at least 13% off the cover price! It's quite a bargain! Shipping and handling is just 50¢ per book.* I understand that accepting the 2 free books and gifts places me under no obligation to buy anything. I can always return a shipment and cancel at any time. Even if I never buy another book, the two free books and gifts are mine to keep forever.

176/376 HDN E5NG

Name _____ (PLEASE PRINT) _____

Address _____ Apt. #

City _____ State/Prov. _____ Zip/Postal Code

Signature (if under 18, a parent or guardian must sign)

Mail to the **Harlequin Reader Service:**
IN U.S.A.: P.O. Box 1867, Buffalo, NY 14240-1867
IN CANADA: P.O. Box 609, Fort Erie, Ontario L2A 5X3

Not valid for current subscribers to Harlequin Presents Larger-Print books.

**Are you a subscriber to Harlequin Presents books
and want to receive the larger-print edition?
Call 1-800-873-8635 today!**

* Terms and prices subject to change without notice. Prices do not include applicable taxes. Sales tax applicable in N.Y. Canadian residents will be charged applicable provincial taxes and GST. Offer not valid in Quebec. This offer is limited to one order per household. All orders subject to approval. Credit or debit balances in a customer's account(s) may be offset by any other outstanding balance owed by or to the customer. Please allow 4 to 6 weeks for delivery. Offer available while quantities last.

Your Privacy: Harlequin Books is committed to protecting your privacy. Our Privacy Policy is available online at www.eHarlequin.com or upon request from the Reader Service. From time to time we make our lists of customers available to reputable third parties who may have a product or service of interest to you. If you would prefer we not share your name and address, please check here. ☐

Help us get it right—We strive for accurate, respectful and relevant communications. To clarify or modify your communication preferences, visit us at www.ReaderService.com/consumerchoice.

HPLP10R

HARLEQUIN®

A Romance

FOR EVERY MOOD™

Spotlight on
Heart & Home

Heartwarming romances
where love can happen
right when you least expect it.

See the next page to enjoy a sneak peek
from Silhouette Special Edition®,
a Heart and Home series.

*Introducing McFARLANE'S PERFECT BRIDE
by USA TODAY bestselling author Christine Rimmer,
from Silhouette Special Edition®.*

Entranced. Captivated. Enchanted.

Connor sat across the table from Tori Jones and couldn't help thinking that those words exactly described what effect the small-town schoolteacher had on him. He might as well stop trying to tell himself he wasn't interested. He was powerfully drawn to her.

Clearly, he should have dated more when he was younger.

There had been a couple of other women since Jennifer had walked out on him. But he had never been entranced. Or captivated. Or enchanted.

Until now.

He wanted her—*her,* Tori Jones, in particular. Not just someone suitably attractive and well-bred, as Jennifer had been. Not just someone sophisticated, sexually exciting and discreet, which pretty much described the two women he'd dated after his marriage crashed and burned.

It came to him that he…he *liked* this woman. And that was new to him. He liked her quick wit, her wisdom and her big heart. He liked the passion in her voice when she talked about things she believed in.

He liked *her.* And suddenly it mattered all out of proportion that she might like him, too.

Was he losing it? He couldn't help but wonder. Was he cracking under the strain—of the soured economy, the McFarlane House setbacks, his divorce, the scary changes in his son? Of the changes he'd decided he needed to make in his life and himself?

Strangely, right then, on his first date with Tori Jones, he didn't care if he just might be going over the edge. He was having a great time—having *fun,* of all things—and he didn't want it to end.

Is Connor finally able to admit his feelings to Tori,
and are they reciprocated?
Find out in McFARLANE'S PERFECT BRIDE
by USA TODAY bestselling author Christine Rimmer.
Available July 2010,
only from Silhouette Special Edition®.

Bestselling Harlequin Presents® author

Penny Jordan

brings you an exciting new trilogy...

Needed:
THE WORLD'S MOST
ELIGIBLE
BILLIONAIRES

Three penniless sisters:
how far will they go to save the ones they love?

Lizzie, Charley and Ruby refuse to drown in their debts.
And three of the richest, most ruthless men in the world
are about to enter their lives. Pure, proud but penniless,
how far will these sisters go to save the ones they love?

Look out for

Lizzie's story—THE WEALTHY GREEK'S
CONTRACT WIFE, July

Charley's story—THE ITALIAN DUKE'S
VIRGIN MISTRESS, August

Ruby's story—MARRIAGE: TO CLAIM HIS TWINS,
September

www.eHarlequin.com

HP12927